The Rest of the Story

The Rest of the Story

Why Would He Do This?

Nancy A. Parks

THE REST OF THE STORY
WHY WOULD HE DO THIS?

Copyright © 2020 Nancy A. Parks.

All rights reserved. No part of this book may be used or reproduced by any means, graphic, electronic, or mechanical, including photocopying, recording, taping or by any information storage retrieval system without the written permission of the author except in the case of brief quotations embodied in critical articles and reviews.

Scripture taken from the NEW AMERICAN STANDARD BIBLE®, Copyright © 1960, 1962, 1963, 1968, 1971, 1972, 1973, 1975, 1977, 1995 by The Lockman Foundation. Used by permission.

iUniverse books may be ordered through booksellers or by contacting:

iUniverse
1663 Liberty Drive
Bloomington, IN 47403
www.iuniverse.com
844-349-9409

Because of the dynamic nature of the Internet, any web addresses or links contained in this book may have changed since publication and may no longer be valid. The views expressed in this work are solely those of the author and do not necessarily reflect the views of the publisher, and the publisher hereby disclaims any responsibility for them.

Any people depicted in stock imagery provided by Getty Images are models, and such images are being used for illustrative purposes only. Certain stock imagery © Getty Images.

ISBN: 978-1-6632-1201-6 (sc)
ISBN: 978-1-6632-1202-3 (e)

Print information available on the last page.

iUniverse rev. date: 11/04/2020

Contents

The Story of Zebedee 1
The Leper Man 17
Jesus The Man.. 27
Anna's Story 43
Matthew.. 65
The Testimony 89
This is Love.. 103

MATTHEW 4:21-22 & 10:2

Going on from there, he saw two brothers James, the son of Zebedee, and his brother John. They were in a boat with their father Zebedee, preparing their nets. Jesus called them, and immediately they left the boat and their father and followed Him.

The Story of Zebedee

Matthew 4: (21-22)

Zebedee lay in the dark before getting up and starting His day. It was early hours before anyone other than the fishermen were awake. So early the sky was black with the night and the stars still sharp points of light in the sky. Zebedee was a Godly hardworking man. He was a strong family man, with strong political views, yet not one to follow every rumor that came on the wind. Undeniably, politics were as much a part of his life as breathing. The Hebrews' hatred of the Romans knew no bounds, so something was always stirring. Rumors here, talk there, and underlying it all, was the talk of the Messiah who would come and rid Israel of the abomination of foreign government. Someday Israel would rule Israel. The Jews, after all, were God's chosen people, in that they were "The PEOPLE OF THE ONE GOD." However, Zebedee for one had not forgotten that the prophets had said that one day even the Gentiles would become one with God. He shook his head, thinking that such a mystery was beyond his understanding. Just how God was going to accomplish this, he had no idea.

His mind wandered back to an earlier hour when the Lord had awakened him by calling his name ever so softly. Their conversations were Zebedee's favorite part of the day or night as the case might be. Yet this time when the Lord departed Zebedee had the strangest feeling that his world, in that moment in time had somehow shifted on its axis. It would never be the same again. He called himself fanciful but he'd spent time with the Lord before and this time it was simply different in ways he couldn't grasp. It was still a sweet, gentle wondrously intimate conversation, the sharing of one heart with another. Yet, when it was finished, he was left with a sense of expectancy. He had no idea how or what or even when but something was about to change. The freshening cool breeze reminded him that he needed to be up. It wouldn't do for the boys to arrive at the shore before he did. He gently pushed aside the coverings and quietly eased out of bed, tucking the cover back around his Mary as she slept. He knew she'd had a hard day yesterday and he didn't want to disturb her. As he turned aside to pick up his cloak and sandals, she smiled and with a sigh went back to sleep, blessing him for his thoughtfulness. He tended to his morning absolutions, blessed his household, and moved to the hearth. Lying on the stone border, wrapped in a cloth were the heavy, nourishing grain cakes that Mary made daily for the household. He swirled the honey stick around in the little pot pulling out the golden sweetness onto his grain cake. His grandchildren had found a hive last month and they were still reaping the rewards of that find.

As he stepped outside, the wind picked up into a steady breeze, his body predictably chooses this moment to unwind. Zebedee reached up to the stars with his big-calloused hands, stretching every fiber of his being. The fresh air flooded into his lungs, and then it moved downward as if the air had the need to reach down into every part of his body, he always ended the exercise with a wide smile and thus began his day.

He walked down the trail, worn deep into the soil by many feet over the years. Earlier this spring, it had turned into a little creek, gathering all the little runnels of water from the spring rains and sending them rushing down the hillside to become one with the Sea of Galilee. He would have to remember to ask the children to begin gathering stones to lay in the trail so it wouldn't become and another muddy mess, come the autumn rains. Looking up he could see the water, the Sea of Galilee, the big inland sea from which he, his father, his grandfather, and many neighbors had earned their livelihood fishing. The Sea of Galilee could be as capricious and changeable as a young girl just entering into the fullness of life. The sea sometimes reminded him of his Mary when they were both young. She was so much like the sea that

Zebedee had never known from one minute to the next what she might do. She could be calm one minute and then some little bit of wind would fluff up her skirts, and then watch out! You might have a full-blown storm in no time or laughter could light up her soft gray eyes with delight and a twinkling mischief. It had made life interesting as he'd learned through the years to sail with one eye on the wind. He also knew to pay attention and he never took his Sarah or the Sea for granted. No, it didn't pay to ignore either one.

Coming around the bend, his smile grew bigger when he realized he was the first of his group to arrive at the boat. While mending and washing nets yesterday, the boys had bet him that, they would arrive here first. His smile grew even bigger at the thought of them all having to pack him oh so gently home on their shoulders. As he heaved the boat over onto the keel, he chuckled to himself, oh, how he was going to love this!

As he busied himself with the small mast and sail, he heard them coming. They were arguing again, debating the most recent news about this new teacher called Jesus. Simon was convinced that He had to be the Messiah, but then Simon was always sure about everything. He was a big man, broad in the shoulders, taller than anyone else in town, ran his own business, and was very successful with his business. Zebedee drew a deep breath, knowing from the sound of things it was going to be another one of those days.

James and Andrew would be arguing with Simon. John would be calmly chewing over every word, while Caleb and Jacob would be urging them on. Of his own two, Zebedee knew that while John was the youngest and most thoughtful, he was the gentlest in his strength. He often spent considerable time thinking through his opinions, yet once they were established, nothing would move him from his conclusions. James however, loved to argue with just about anyone, on any subject. Zebedee sometimes regretted that he had not had the money to pay for additional schooling for James. Zebedee believed he could have been a great lawyer if only things were different. Looking to the heavens and grinning, he told the Lord, "And if James were a lawyer, I wouldn't have to sit in a boat with him for half the night!"

Smiling he pull his robe over his head, neatly folded it, and slid it into a basket under his seat to keep it dry. He had a hard time keeping himself from laughing outright when they all came around the bend and found him sitting at the tiller ready to go. It was grand to see the looks on their faces as they realized he had beaten them to the boat! Maybe the arguing would be tolerable after all. Simon turned and went back down the beach shaking his head and muttering about sleepless old men. Still grinning, the boys pulled off their robes, and together put their shoulders to the sides of the boat and pushed her into the water. When she had enough depth under her, they hauled themselves into the boat, the younger ones going to the oars, Zebedee to the tiller and the others tended the sails. Soon after setting sail, as was his custom Zebedee began to sing, before long James and John joined in, their voices sounding as if each came from the bottom of a barrel. Then Caleb and Jacob would join in with the harmony and so they would pass the night into the morning. Many agreed that they were aptly named the Sons of Thunder. Their voices rose and fell with the strokes of the oars, singing praises and thankfulness to their God. It was a good sound and a good way to spend the day.

Soon they were far enough out from shore and into the deep pools where fish seemed to gather and the cast their nets on the water. Thus, began the day's work, repeating the rhythm until the sun was climbing high into the sky and the last two passes yielded no fish. As they began their return to shore, Zebedee sat quietly watching their progress, thinking that they had made a good catch. Simon and Andrew with their crew were proving to be good partners. They weren't back yet but it wouldn't be long before they were. Zebedee hoped that today there would be enough profit to buy the pretty piece of nice cloth he had seen Mary reverently stroking the other day in the market.

The shoreline was a welcome sight, for Zebedee was tired. His shoulders ached and he's a new blister under the callous on his left hand that stung. But there was still the catch to sort and sell, nets to wash and dry, and today would be a good day to do some mending. Then cleaning the boat and getting it out of the water for the night still would have to be done. He knew it would be afternoon before he finally rested. He could see Mary on the beach with all the different baskets for sorting the fish to sell. She stood tall and slim; her dress pressed by the wind against her legs, her hand shielding her eyes as she stood watch waiting for their return. Mary often spent her days waiting for him to bring the food from the sea. Together, they were all waiting for their daughter's first child, and as soon as Mary caught sight of them, she began waving her white shawl. The men then knew the time for the baby had arrived. When they got close enough to shore, Jacob, her husband fairly flew through the water, sprinting for home with his mother close behind. John grumbled that it wouldn't do him a bit of good and everyone laughed as James reminded him that Mother had banned him from any more deliveries, as he was more nervous than the new mothers! John grinned and sent Jacob's brother Caleb after him, to try to keep him company and out of Mother's way. Although they were shorthanded, they would be better off keeping their hands busy, rather than fretting about their sisters' birth pains. Yes, this was the best place for them. They'd pull the boat into shore, sit in the shade of the sail, and work the time away.

They happily passed the hours mending their nets and doing the other little and big chores that constantly sprung up demanding attention. They were all so preoccupied that they didn't see the Man coming towards them up the beach towards the boat. There was a purpose and direction in His stride. The other watchers could tell He wasn't out for a casual stroll and wondered at His purpose. Wasn't that the carpenter, Jesus of Nazareth, it looked like who they had described. He was that healer and teacher that had the entire country buzzing with speculation and rumor. There was an electric expectation that seemed to make the air crackle with excitement and joy. Delight and anticipation seemed to radiate from Jesus as He walked. Watching, His growing audience paid close attention as He moved down the beach, waiting to see what He would do next.

The day was a glorious spring afternoon. The sky was a deep blue that lightened only marginally near the horizon. It was filled that day with puffs of white clouds that never quite joined but raced each other to be the first across the sky. The wind had died down a bit yet still played with the loose strands of the Man's hair, tossing it here and there, sometimes slapping it against His cheeks when he turned His head to greet someone. The sunlight seemed to surround Him as He walked, glinting off the lighter streaks in His hair. The town on His left teemed with activity. Children played, while older girls watched over them. Older women were doing their washing. Young girls laughed as they hurried up the beach to the cove. The young men called out greetings, as they worked alone or with their fathers. Others gathered and separated the catch of the day, those to be sold, and those to take home. The fishmongers haggled over prices and amounts as they made their bids. All coupled with the good-natured talk and banter that surrounded the shoreline.

The sun, the wind, the slap of the waves on the sand, and the screech of the gulls as they fought for the new contributions to the refuse piles, all-contributing to Jesus's sense of wonder, and sheer delight in the world He and His Father had created. All of these elements, coupled with the excitement of His purpose, formed in Jesus an over whelming joy and thankfulness. This was reflected in His smile and every movement of His body. Jesus turned His face into the wind, again tasting its freshness and reveling in the warmth of the sun on His skin. The tug of the wind flattened His garments to His body as if it were teasing Him, testing its strength while flirting with Him. Jesus was filled with the knowledge that today He would begin to gather to Himself, the Men, and Women who would be His closest companions, and most intimate of friends. These people would give Him both the ultimate in joy, and the greatest in sorrow. These were the ones He would teach and train. With these strong earthy men and devoted women, His Father would build a foundational group that would eventually take His kingdom to every human being on earth. These fishermen were the first fruits. They would be the first to come to know and believe in Him as the Son of God. They were the first to be led out of the separation, the division from their Creator that sin had created. The anticipation set His feet to dancing; He wanted to shout for joy that this day was finally here! Finally, there would be liberty from the curse that had lain on humanity since Adam's failure in the garden. He could begin to eradicate the division between the Creator and His creation. Never again, would there be the impassable barrier of sin between the Triune Godhead and the precious people who were so incredibly loved by their Father. He was here to make the final sacrifice that would forever clear the way for God's beloved children. His face darkened at the thought of the hard times ahead, but it cleared soon as He looked forward to the resulting joy that would be His forever more.

Soon His was abreast of the boats and fishermen who greeted Him in their quiet way, speculation apparent in their eyes. His first appointment was with Simon and Andrew, "And going from there He saw two other brothers James and John the sons of Zebedee in the boat." He stopped in front of Zebedee's boat and simply stood there, expectation in every line of His body. Suddenly Zebedee's eyes lifted and seeing Jesus, he abruptly knew he was looking into the eyes of the Messiah. In that moment of unspoken understanding, several things happened at once. Zebedee nodded his head giving permission to the request in the eyes of Jesus and Jesus called out their names. Lifting their heads, they too looked into His eyes and then flashing a glance at their father; they stood and immediately left the boat to follow Jesus.

As they walked away, Zebedee leaned back against the mast; astonishment crowded all other thoughts from his mind for he knew he had looked into the eyes of Israel's Messiah. He had just given his sons into the care and keeping of the Lord Most High and his spirit soared as the reality of that took root in his heart. He knew that from this time forward everything would be different. As they followed Jesus, Zebedee leaned back against the mast; astonishment crowded all other thoughts from his mind for he knew he had looked into the eyes of Israel's Messiah. He had just given his sons into the care and keeping of the Lord Most High and his spirit soared as the reality of that took root in his heart. He knew that for this time forward nothing would ever be the same again, not for his family, his religion, or his people. Oh, the joy of it all! Our Messiah is here! The thought rocked him once again but he instinctively knew the expectations of his fellow countrymen and the realities being instituted by that extraordinary young man were vastly different. God was indeed doing something different, but as always, He was doing it His way. It would not be the way of man or of religion nor of politics, but the way of our sovereign God. With a huge grin splitting his face, Zebedee chuckled to himself as he thought, 'Oh my yes, how things will change."

Indeed, and change they did, and are still changing as God reveals more and more of His secrets every minute. Whenever Jesus enters the picture, He changes us. He rocks our world and sets it on its ear every time. Many believers see Jesus as a passive, grave, kindly man, who sacrificed His life as a poor innocent lamb whose only purpose was to get us into heaven. Well I'm sorry but that is not all He did. He was beaten until He no longer even looked like a human being. His body was ripped to shreds by a cat of nine tails each end fitted with sharpened pieces of metal that ripped and tore every piece of skin, muscle and ligament it touched, scouring down to the bone of the victim; from the back of their head to the calves of the legs. Then He was ridiculed and beaten and shoved again until He fell, unable to carry the wooden beam they had laid on His ripped, bloody, and tattered body. And in that moment of incredible agony, every disease and sickness known to man was inflicted on His body. But it was not yet done, they then took Him to a 4 foot hole in the ground where a beaten bloody beam lay on the ground and they took the cross beam and tired down His hands and drove spikes into His wrist bones then moved the main beam and attached it to the tall one shoving His knees up just enough to keep Him suffering while He tried to gain some relief for His lungs. Then came the sin, every sin imaginable and some beyond human comprehension, from every human being ever born to everyone who was still to live. He did this, He suffered through this so that you and I can have a relationship with our God, our Father, our Everything, and so you can live with Him forever. No more tears, no more hurt, no more fear, no more despair, nothing that would cause you any kind of hurt, because you will be with God who won't allow it in His realm.

Jesus is the life inside of us; He is that very essence of life that bubbles and sparkles with an effervescence that blows the lid off our rigid, manmade religious thinking and doing. He pops out, exploding our oh so finite concepts of God, of who He is, what He can and cannot do. Our infinite all knowing, all capable God, is who we seem determined to stuff down into this little tiny box with a lid of our making. We keep Him confined and contained until our minds become numb to the reality of who it is that we are really dealing with. We deny His majesty, His Righteousness, His Holiness, and His sovereignty. But most of all we deny our need to measure up. Jesus isn't some stiff, ridged person, He created the universe in which we live with all of its abundant diversity that we have barely begun to scrape the surface of seeing and understanding. This is the one who helped build creation, Jesus was its creator He was its very author. Jesus is flexibility, change, the unexpected, the wonder, the awe of all creation. He is the essential essence of our lives. When you hear that little voice in the back of your mind or you feel that unaccountable nudge to think about, to learn about this Jesus. Jump out of your supposedly safe little boat, this seemingly secure confined, structured little place in line, and join in with Him for the grandest adventure of your life. It may not always be easy but life never is. Run to Him, throw your arms around Him and hold on for the dearness of life and never leave His side, for He will never, ever leave you!

Understand that He longs for relationship with you He wants you to tell Him everything and anything for He will do the same for you. There is nothing of Himself He would withhold from you. He will delight in sharing with you the sweet confidences of a beloved and trusted friend. He wants to be there for you, to comfort, console, teach, guide, and don't forget He loves to laugh with you and for you all the days of your life. He wants you to allow Him to live and move through you, your hands soothing, your eyes crying in sympathy, your ears listening to heart wrenching grief and need. Your body stepping in and doing what He would do for He lives and breathes thru our being. He is here through you. So, when He calls drop everything and join with Him, you will never ever regret fully living your life with Him.

GO IN GOD'S PEACE! AMEN!

MATTHEW 8:1-3

WHEN He came down from the mountainside, large crowds followed him. A man with leprosy came and knelt before him, and said, "Lord, if you are willing, you can make me clean." Jesus reached out his hand and touched the man. "I am willing." He said. "Be clean!" Immediately he was cured of his leprosy.

LUKE 5:12-13

The Leper Man

Long ago, there lived a man. Now this was a man as any other man. He was not especially good to look upon, nor was there any particular talent that made him stand out from other men. He was only about five foot three, with a dark sharp face. His nose was hooked and pointy, and his mouth a thin slash across his face. Perhaps his best features were his eyes. Although they could be shifty and cunning, when he laughed you could see that he laughed clear into the depth of his soul. However, laughter had been gone a long time from his countenance. What were left were the ravages of leprosy. This man was the Leper.

He had long ago lost contact with any member of his family. If they did chance to meet anywhere, they covered their faces and turned way, refusing to even meet his eyes. He was the Leper man, the unclean one, and the one that was never allowed contact with healthy people because of the law and because of their fear of contamination. He lived his life on the outer fringes of humanity, never a part of life, or community, never welcomed, never wanted. When people passed by, he saw the horror rise up in their eyes. He watched as their nostrils caught the scent of his flesh as it rotted away. He saw the fear and sickness come up into their faces, as their minds and stomachs rejected the reality of the leprosy. They would turn and hurry away from him, as if even the smell of the disease carried its own contamination.

For the Leper man, even the basics of survival were hard to come by. Food was given by the charitable. He could only get enough if he could get there first, but that didn't happen very often. There was rarely enough to go around, as most went to the beggars who, while on the outside of society were not considered unclean. Unlike the Leper man and others like him, they often had homes. They had human contact and they belonged. His clothing, if it could be called that, was as filthy as his body. The rags hung from his frame in tattered layers, looking as if he had simply covered the holes and worn spots with just another layer. He looked like a slow moving mass of dirty rags, slowly shuffling its way down the road. Each slow dragging movement created its own little cloud, coating him with yet another layer of dirt with each painful step.

In this dry country, where water was liquid gold, it was hard for him and the other Lepers to find a place where they were allowed to draw water even to drink. He used to long to bathe, to have warm, clean water surround him and to have the soap scrub away the accumulated grime and filth that covered his skin as if it were a protective shell holding his body together. Sadly, there was no such place that would allow lepers to bathe, after all, who would be willing to allow *his* unclean hand to touch anything of theirs? Besides he was a Leper, one of the rejects of humanity, some believing them to be cursed by God. Moreover, even he began to think that if he tried scrubbing the grime away he'd see the rest of his body float away in the water. Living day today was very difficult for the Leper man.

There had been little in his life to give him hope, until last week when he'd heard the elders talking. To them, he was a pile of rags with bones poking out, so they freely talked as they passed him by, giving him a wide berth as they pretended he didn't exist. These great religious ones were so sure he'd committed some terrible sin or blasphemy to become a Leper. He hadn't, he just knew in his heart he hadn't. However, the elders were talking about this new 'Rabbi', the teacher called Jesus, saying He was performing miracles of healing. He fed thousands of people at a time, the blind could see and the lame could walk. Demoniacs were set free. Infirmities disappeared. There were even rumors that He raised the dead.

At first, the Leper man thought that this was just more talk. His people were always talking about some new miracle worker that would soon turn into the Messiah and save Israel. As far as he could see, the only thing they ever turned into were charlatans and thieves running for their lives. However, this one had the religious crowd worried. They said He was different. He would heal anyone, rich or poor. He wouldn't accept money or property for healing them either He just did it. They said that many times He told those he healed to keep silent, except to give God the glory. The Leper man then shook his head just thinking about it. That would be a wonder all by itself. For how could you possibly be expected to be quiet about being healed, having your life back, about being fully alive once more? He truly didn't know how that could be done.

That's what stared the daydreams, the thoughts swirling about in his mind as he walked slowly from one place to another, ever searching for the necessities. The dreams created in him an aching need that was almost impossible to bear. He found himself constantly thinking about what it would be like to not hurt, to not stink; to stand upright on feet able to support you without a crutch and not be all shrunk down with constant pain and a hopeless misery that never ended until the day you died. To know that once again you have a family and friends, to actually belong to someone, somewhere. To know you were free to touch and be touched by another human being.

Oh the incredible, indescribable joy of that moment, think of it! To be made whole! To have all the pieces that had fallen off or been destroyed, that had rotted away,

The Rest of the Story

to have them come back whole and strong. It would be so indescribably sweet, so God given miraculous. They said that this Jesus of Nazareth simply commands it and it's done, just that fast.

The Leper man shook his head, telling himself it was all just a dream. It certainly was never going to happen to him, he was foolish to even hope it would. With a nasty snort, he thought about the other healers he'd dealt with. Most of the time, he couldn't even get close to them. If they saw him approaching, they'd run. When they were far enough away, they'd pelt him with rocks. He didn't think he'd survive another stoning.

Keeping his head down, he pushed on through the heat of the day, trying to get on to the next charitable place that might have food. He'd heard that sometimes there was even enough for the Lepers. Besides, it was mid-day and he rather liked having the hot, dusty road to himself. No one else was likely to be out, and he wouldn't have to keep shouting, "UNCLEAN! UNCLEAN!" every step of the way. He considered stopping in the little bit of shade for a while, but he continued on, shuffling past the high bushes that lined the bend in the road. He kept his head down so he could watch his feet; he couldn't afford to fall again. When suddenly, he heard running footsteps and before he could turn away or call out, "UNCLEAN!' A smiling young man with the joy of life on His face, jumped down from the hillside path onto the road directly in front of him. The Leper man was so astonished, he looked straight up into His eyes, and what he saw there made him wish he never had to look away. For in His eyes, he saw the laughter disappear, and instead of horror and disgust appearing as the stranger took in the sights and smells before Him, the Leper man saw tears of loving compassion welling up in His eyes. His eyes filled with a yearning to help that overwhelmed the Leper man as he stood there, frozen on the dusty road way. Time itself seemed to stand still as the stranger looked into his soul. The sun became brighter. The very air caught its breath, as if it too was waiting to see what would happen next. For in that moment the SON OF GOD, in the form of a man, had come face to face with a portion of the hideous results of mankind's rejection of His Father. Suddenly the Leper knew who this was. This was Jesus of Nazareth, the Rabbi, the healer the entire countryside was talking about. Looking into Jesus' eyes he knew that this was the one, the only one that could make him complete again and he "…bowed down to Him saying, Lord if you are willing you can make me clean." Then Jesus did something that no other human being on the face of the earth had done for years beyond measure. He stretched out His hand and He touched him, and then simply said, "I am willing…be cleansed. And immediately his leprosy was cleansed."

Hardly believing what his mind and body were telling him. Levi touched his face where the bone had melted away in the agony of the disease. Once again, there was bone. The eye socket that had been empty for so many years was full and he could really see. He realized that all his fingers were restored to his hands and his skin no longer had the dreaded patches of white that were the terrifying signs of Leprosy. He looked down and his legs were straight, and he had toes! He could walk, unsupported by the broken limbs of trees, and even to run and jump if he wanted to. Tears of joy and unimaginable thanksgiving to God, streamed down his face, as he struggled to understand that he had been given back his life. He was not only cleansed but he was restored. He was ALIVE! HE WAS WHOLE! His body was complete. He could have life once more not just existence, all because of this man they called Jesus. This Jesus standing before him had this incomprehensible loving compassion for him, Levi. Jesus has willingly given him back his life neither asking nor demanding anything in return.

That is what He does, that is what He's like. That is what He is willing to do for the Leper man and for you. Jesus was and is moved by compassion that stems from a love we truly and rarely deeply understand. However, compassion is not a passive emotion that just sits inside and you simply feel it. That's more often just pity or sympathy. But true compassion wells up from your gut deep down inside of you. It moves you, it forces you to move, to do something, anything you can to help, to understand, to solve. It's not compassion unless it moves you to do *something as it does with Jesus.* Jesus didn't just heal Levi He touched him He physically put His hand on a person with Leprosy which is only the worst possible thing you could do to yourself, it was that contagious and that feared, Jesus touched him even before He healed him. His loving compassion knew what was needed first and foremost. Please consider reaching out to people touch them, hug them and let them feel the love of God flow thru you into them. And when compassion moves you please, please don't shut it down move with it and do whatever God directs you to do. Loving Compassion is the motivating foundation for everything in God's kingdom. Begin to measure your behavior and your motives against His standard of Love. By doing this you will begin a life of Kingdom power, based on a foundation of compassionate love that mirrors who Jesus Christ is. Because really isn't that the goal, to be as much like Him as we can with the assistance of the Holy Spirit? Go with God and pay attention when moved by compassion for in loving compassion our Jesus moves with us.

JOHN 8:28

JOHN 10: 30-38,

John 15:9

Jesus The Man

Sitting on a rock at the edge of the meadow, He watched the people as they gathered their belongings in preparation for going home after a long day of listening to Jesus teach. The sun was sinking into the western horizon, painting the sky with spectacular colors of pink, orange, and scarlet, all on a canvas of brilliant blue. It seemed only moments before it melted into the rich bluish purples of the evening sky. It was a magnificent sight that Jesus loved watching. As each day began and ended with this symphony of colors that delighted His soul and soothed His spirit. As He sat watching the sky, He noticed that a few people still lingered, seemingly waiting to talk with Him. They seemed hesitant, as if actually afraid to approach Him for fear of rejection or their questions would somehow be unseemly to Him the Rabbi. He smiled and waved them forward indicating His willingness to speak with them. Out of the corner of His eye, He saw Peter frown and make a move towards Him to chase them off. However, Jesus stopped him with a shake of His head. He turned to the young couples as they approached Him, greeting them all with a smile and a chuckle when a small child escaped her mother's grasp and threw her little arms around His legs, burying her face in the folds of His garments. Jesus laughingly held the child's shoulders and sank down to be on her level. This almost proved to be an upset because the child seeing this new opportunity to be even closer to her new friend flung her arms around Jesus' neck that almost rolled him over backwards. The poor mother was appalled to see her daughter behave this way with the great Teacher and Healer. She'd even heard it said that He could be the Messiah! He astonished her by laughing with delight, and sitting back on the ground, He pulled the child into His lap, and gestured to the adults to be seated. He hugged little Suzanna, loving the feel of the warm trusting little body in His arms. She snuggled close to Him laying her cheek against His chest listening to His beating heart and the gentle cadence of His voice, content to simply be with the kind man who was so obviously delighted with her.

However, it was clear to any observer that the adults were equally taken by this man who so willingly spoke with them. He was definitely not like any of the other teachers who were around at the time. This teacher really listened and talked to them instead of at them. He didn't make them feel ignorant or foolish when He

The Rest of the Story

answered their questions either. He included the women in the discussion, which amazed the women even more than the men. When Sarah dared give her hesitant opinion regarding a point in scripture Jesus just nodded in agreement and even told her she had made a good point. All too soon, they realized that it was past time to go, the men reluctantly standing, clearly loathed to go. They helped their wives gather all the belongings while Jesus stood cradling the now sleeping Suzanna in His arms. He was looking at her as if it would hurt to hand her back to her parents. Then He sighed and ever so gently kissed her forehead holding His cheek against the side of her face as He spoke words of blessing over her. The parents, startled that He would bless their wayward child were completely taken aback when they saw the tears running down the teachers face as He stood there holding their little one. The moment soon passed as He blessed them too and sent them on their way. It had truly been a day they would never forget.

He stood there quietly watching them go, feeling as though all the energy had suddenly drained from His body. He scrubbed His hands over His face as if trying to rub some sort of life back into His tired mind and body. He was very tired and could hardly wait to sit and simply rest. When He turned and looked back up the hill, He saw His friends had built a fire. He could smell meat cooking, and thought that one of them must have snared a few quail, and while they roasted, the men sat around the fire talking about the day's events. He stood for a moment savoring the smell, realizing His tiredness was combined with a feeling of deep satisfaction as He mentally reviewed the day. He also checked in with His Father for a brief moment for further instructions and He smiled in relief to hear He would soon be resting in His Father's arms.

He kept a running conversation with His Father just as you do with anyone you worked with side by side. They discussed everything from how to help the growing numbers of people seeking Jesus, wanting to know more and more of God the Father, to where to stop for the noonday rest. Jesus made no move that didn't have His Father's will behind it. Their conversation usually started the first thing in the morning when He first awoke and ended when He laid His head in His Father's lap at night to sleep.

Sighing, He wished He were already up in the hill, with his camp set up, and not having to move another inch. He and His Father were together minute by minute during the day, but they needed more than that, they needed this coming time to be private and intimate with each other. Most days were so full that He never had a moment to Himself; there was always someone or something that needed His attention. Jesus knew He had to have time, time to hear and think about

His Father's input in order to process all that happened daily in His life. Besides that, there was a yearning for His Father at a level that began in the very depths of His being. The need for His Father was a draw on His spirit that was difficult to explain. At its worst, it was like a devastating homesickness for a person instead of a place but that was there too in the background. At its best, it was an aching need that never faded away. The need to be in His Father's presence was never completely satisfied, for there was an aching sweetness in His Father's companionship that permeated every part of His being. The Father's love and comfort washed away the grime of negatives in the world in which he lived; simply being in His presence brought contentment and a huge sense of serene safety that nothing or no one on earth could come close to replicating. In joy, in sorrow, in troubled times, in confusion and despair, He was the one who could give Jesus the balm to restore and make bearable the emotions of His heart.

As he walked up the hill towards the fire, he thought about the people He had talked with throughout the day. He found Himself shaking His head in renewed surprise at the number of people who could not conceive of their Creator laughing, dancing, crying, or even keeping time to music of the drums and pipes. He wondered at their inability to see their heavenly Father as anyone other than some huge presence you should be terrified of attracting His notice. For, were they not made in *His image in His* likeness *didn't they understand that for them to have laughter and joy He had to have it first?* Over time, religious traditions had robbed their minds of truly understanding their own unique likeness to their Father, and it grieved His soul. Religion had not only robbed the children, but it had stolen from the Father the fullness of His magnificence in the eyes of the world.

Jesus walked towards the fire, trying to walk at a slight angle so the fire would light His path. He came to stand beside Peter and put His hand on his shoulder to let him now he was there. He waited for an opening in the conversation and told them He would spend the night in the hills and that He would see them in the morning. They all knew they couldn't persuade Him to stay but Peter couldn't resist reminding Him to be careful and to build Himself a good fire. John scooped up some ashes into a hollowed-out horn, and rolled a few live coals into it, with a little more ash. He handed Him the horn and grinning, quickly wrapped a few pieces of the meat and a big chunk of fresh bread into a cloth for His evening meal. Jesus smiled in return, thanked him, and quietly bid them goodnight. He then picked up a lite torch and walked away into the night seeking the solace and companionship of His Father.

He headed towards a nice little U-shaped spot in the rocks that had a sandy floor and not too far from

The Rest of the Story

a natural spring. He walked, being careful of the path and after a time, He heard an animal move off into the brush, and a moment later heard the sound of the spring gently bubbling out of the ground. He decided to fill His water skin and move on away from the water so His presence wouldn't keep the animals from coming in for a drink. He knelt down beside the still waters of the pool, ducked His hands into the water and splashed the cool clean water onto His face then quickly filled His water skin. When He looked up, the moon was a thin sliver in the night sky and the stars looked close enough for Him to reach out and touch. A smile of quick delight crossed His face as He watched a falling star burn its way across the heavens. It felt as if His Father were greeting Him with a wave of His hand across the night sky. He finished tying off the neck of the water skin, slung it across His shoulder, and moved to stand up. Unfortunately, the kneeling had made His tired muscles knot up and as He tried to stand, He staggered and fell hard against the rock wall on His right slamming His upper arm into a jagged part of the rock. As the pain crossed down His arm, He closed His eyes absorbing the shock. Immediately He felt His Father's hand and the soothing presence of the Holy Spirit. The pain left and regaining His balance, He straightened up to feel the little pop of the vertebrae as it moved back into place in His back. That faint achy, burning feeling between

His shoulder blades that had haunted Him all day was now gone. Smiling to Himself and walking slowly, He moved away from the pool looking for the old camping place and picking up firewood as he found it along the trail. When He finally arrived, He grunted with relief. Picking up tender and small sticks, He gathered enough to start His fire. He was grateful for the coals John had given Him and using them He lite His fire and sat down with a sigh of relief. He moved a bit, settling His body deeper into the sand, removing a larger pebble here and there and finally wrapping His robe closer to His body, He opened His food and began His conversation with His Father.

They talked about yesterday morning, laughing together as Jesus recounted the foot race between Him and Nathaniel. Nathaniel had said he could get to the olive tree before Jesus could, so they drew a line in the dirt of the road and Matthew yelled Go! Off they went running all out as the others cheered them on; Nathaniel had won, but not by much. It had been such fun to simply run full out, as He often did as a child.

He reminded His Father of the group of travelers He and His friends had joined when they stopped for a rest alongside the road. They talked about the people, how they hurt and despaired under Roman rule; how they felt they had no hope of ever being free. The Romans took their money and anything else they could get away with. Jesus spoke about the people's poverty, not only the lack of finances but also the poverty of their minds, bodies, and spirits. As He spoke of the children, tears ran down His face as He spoke of those who had been demon possessed or physically sick. The Father talked of the adults who were forever chained to the need to always be in control. The sorrow in His voice as He talked of those who lived with fear in addition, a lack of trust in the goodness and love of their Heavenly Father brought even more tears to the eyes of Jesus. That same fear bound these people to the harshest of taskmasters. Doomed always to a life of fixing and managing, trying with everything in them to make things and people turn out the way they needed them to be; unknowingly trying to be god of the situation or the circumstance.

Jesus knew and understood the problems people had to cope with; He had to deal with the exact same ones as they did. He and His Father talked about them daily, sometimes minute by minute. He knew the pounding power of sin as well as its gentle insidious pull, every waking moment. He fought it every day at every turn. Jesus had to constantly, continuously; choose between what He knew to be His Father's heart and the desires of His own flesh. Temptations lurked around every corner, always ready to trip Him or deceive Him into falling. Every sin and iniquity imaginable followed Him like a pack of ravenous wolves. Tiredness could make it so easy to choose to be rude; the heat of the day gave opportunity for inconsiderate behavior. Religion can easily excuse being judgmental and critical. He and His Father talked about how easy it was for Him to fall back into His own reasoning and intellectual understanding. He knew how easy it could be to put in just a word here or critical judgement there, comparing instead of praying for compassion and understanding. Jesus too, found it incredibly easy to allow His infallible mind to work out the issues of His life instead of taking them to His Father just as we could do. However, the bottom line was that Adam and Eve saw nothing wrong with being 'AS GOD,' with all of its ramifications. Jesus, The Holy Spirit, and the Father are always aware of how easy we find it to follow the flesh instead of the Spirit.

Jesus told His Father about the troubling facts of man's religious opinions that have become tradition instead of following the intent of the Father's heart. Admittedly walking in the instruction of His sweet Spirit could be hard when battling the flesh at the same time. Jesus had discovered in Himself a desire to follow the rules whether they were made up by Him or were made for Him by His culture and religion of the day. He found Himself fighting against the pull to do or think in terms of those humanistic rules instead of obeying the Spirit of His Father's heart. Sometimes He told His Father it could be so easy to just let it happen, to let His guard down, to relax, to ignore the Spirit and just fall into the flow of the world around Him, but when it came down to it, He just couldn't let Himself follow through there was too much at stake. However, sometimes to simply say whatever came to mind, to edit nothing, to behave as the world did was truly a temptation. However, He would then have to face the consequences of His choices. He'd have to look into their eyes and see the pain, the wounding, and the knowledge of the Messiah's betrayal. He would have to acknowledge that He could now do nothing to ease the torment of their separation from the Father. For Him to have to face the people, to see their fragile hopes die an ugly death was more than He could imagine coping with. He cringed inside with the conviction of what that would do to His Father and the Holy Spirit. He couldn't, He wouldn't do that. He knew He was their only chance and would do nothing to jeopardize that, no matter what the cost.

On through the night they talked, the Father so close as to seem a physical part of Jesus as He sat there looking out into the night. Eventually wariness overcame His need to talk and He laid His head in His Father's lap, and went to sleep, His Father keeping watch through the night.

He awoke when in rolling over, the sun hit Him in the eyes, and for a moment, He just laid there enjoying the feel of the warmth of the sun on His face. He watched the strange little things that appeared on the inside of His eyelids as He lay savoring the sun and the feelings of being rested and relaxed. Soon though He rolled back out of the sun and lay there thinking about yesterday and restarted, His conversation with His Father, He spoke of the people He had been able to help, mourned, and grieved over the ones that wouldn't accept His help.

They talked about the men who had been sent from the temple and from other sects and factions within Jerusalem. These professed scholars of the Mosaic scriptures had stood on the fringes of the crowd or even mingled among the people trying to discredit Jesus. Their arms crossed, their faces openly sneering, and hostile, murmuring when He spoke. Later, some posed questions intended to trap or discredit Him. These great and so-called knowledgeable men, their arrogant assumptions all mixed with this disdainful attitude of intellectual conceit often tried the patience of Jesus past endurance. Their rational was that surely, men with their training and their commanding knowledge of scripture were far superior to this carpenter from of all places, Nazareth. This Man had no education or training in the temple, who had never spent a single day or even an hour with the great teachers of the day. How could He possibly know anything about God? "Impossible!" they declared repeatedly to themselves and anyone else who would listen. Others inserted themselves into the crowds to ask the people "meaningful questions" meant to bring division, or at least lead the innocent to doubt. These were the sly ones, yes, they were attempting to discredit Him, but they were also seeking to destroy with intellectual conceit, what the Holy Spirit was building into the hearts of the people. As these elders would gather, their underlying hatred and fear spilled over as they snapped and snarled at each other like dogs from different packs. They lived their lives in a constant scramble to discredit each other as well as this upstart, this unlearned carpenter, this Jesus, who to their minds had absolutely no business trying to teach anyone about something as majestically difficult as God. The hearts of both Father and Son grieved for those who were snared by the unrighteous words and motives of these men.

As He got ready to leave Jesus made sure the last tendril of smoke was doused with water and left His little sanctuary in order. He gathered His things into His pack refilled his water skin and headed down the path to His friends. He walked this day and every day with His Father and the Holy Spirit over an earth that had once been theirs alone each knowing that the other was only a thought away. Taking comfort in the knowledge that these close, intimate, times were always available. Jesus walked this earth in the same way you do, He experienced the same trials, the same tribulations, the same choices. He chose to make His Father God the Lord of His life, He chose to live according to His Father's commandments and His wishes, He chose, He chose. He however, made all the right choices so that when You are confronted with these same choices you can look to Him for help, for comfort, and understanding. He knows how hard it is for you. He knows every intimate detail of your life. Look at Psalms the whole book if you need reassurance about how well He knows you! Every day you spend with Him will show you just how much He does understand. He will love you through every step you take whether backwards or forwards, if you will just let Him. Get to know the God who made you to be so much like Him. That act was extremely personal on His part, so isn't it time you got personal with Jesus. I hope and pray that you do! AMEN!

LUKE 8:43-47

And a woman having an issue of blood of twelve years, which had spent all her living upon physicians, neither could be healed of any. Came behind Him, and touched the border of his garment: and immediately her issue of blood stanched. And Jesus said, "Who touched me?" when all denied, Peter and they that were with him said, "Master, the multitude throng thee, and sayest thou, who touched me?"

Anna's Story

She sat at the table staring out the doorway watching the children as they played in the courtyard. Sitting there in the cool of the house with the door swung back and fastened to the wall, she smiled at some of their antics, frowned when they picked on the littlest ones and became angry when they were unkind or mean to each other. However, through it all she rarely moved. She simply had no strength to go to the little ones with scratched knees or to scold the ones who were unkind. Besides, she was considered unclean and was banned from interacting with anyone. Her neighbor's oldest child left to do chores and soon all of the children would be gone from the area, called home for the evening meal and chores.

She supposed she should prepare something for herself to eat, but she didn't she could not summon the energy to move. She was so very tired these days. She would have given just about anything if it was the kind of fatigue that came from completing a day's hard work but it wasn't. It was fatigue that wore you down little by little, day by day. Slowly suffocating every desire or inclination to accomplish anything but the most basic responsibilities to even think about simply moving was tiring. Tears slowly formed in her eyes as the unrelenting feelings of hopelessness and despair threatened to overwhelm her once again. She had been told by the priests that God was punishing her. However, for what, she couldn't begin to imagine. The priests said there was sin in her life. For why else would she be afflicted this long? They said that the sin must be some dark and secret thing she was unwilling to confess and make right before God. She felt shamed and embarrassed whenever she thought of the priests and their attitudes towards her. She shook her head in confusion, wondering what it could possibly be that she had done. Shaking her head again, she angrily cast aside the tormenting questions that played havoc with her belief in her God's integrity and her faith in Him. It wasn't as if she hadn't searched herself. She had repeatedly, confessed to everything she could imagine that she might have done wrong. Yet in spite of this, the bleeding never stopped and it was getting worse. She had now been bleeding for twelve long miserable years.

Anna continued to sit quietly, thinking back over the years. Her father had been moderately wealthy and had arranged a marriage for her when she was only ten. At that time, Simon had seemed horribly old at twenty to her ten-year-old self. She had cried for days. She was married shortly after she became a woman; she smiled faintly at the thought. Theirs had not been a passionate or romantic marriage. It was as common as the days were long and before the children were born it was often boring. She was a healthy, vigorous fourteen-year old, with more time on her hands than she could often fill. As was common, they had been married out of mutual need, not out of mutual love. He had needed a wife to bear him heirs and she needed a husband to provide for her. There was courtesy and kindness in the marriage and if there was no grand passion, there was at least no strife. For Anna those first two years, seemed almost monotonous in their sameness until in the second year she became pregnant with their first child. She gave birth at fifteen and was a long difficult delivery it was also the beginning of her life for her, she was now a busy young mother delighting in her son. Simon was also delighted with his son and with Anna. The baby's first act was to grab hold of his father's finger and wrap himself around his heart. The household now took on a life of its own. Not only was there peace but now also joy. Only a short time later Anna became pregnant again. She and Simon were both over joyed, in due time, there was a tiny little girl. However, for Anna not all was well. The delivery was even longer and harder, and Simon feared for their lives before it was over. Fortunately, their little girl was a healthy and happy child that adored her father and he her. However, as the child grew and thrived Anna did not, she continued to bleed long after she should have been done, and she grew weaker. Simon called in numerous physicians and soon after no results called in the priests who were no help at all, only making things worse with flung out guilt and unwarranted shame. Finally, after over 9 months the bleeding slowed but never really stopped. This just added to Anna's problems as this kept her in a constant state of being unclean according to the laws of Moses. This limited her contact with people and causing problems at home for Simon and the children not to mention what it did to Anna.

Over time, Simon tired of seeking ways to live normally with Anna. She so appreciated his efforts but after three years, he had finally given her a writ of divorce. Which broke her heart feeling shamed, abandoned, and panicked, as she now had no way to support herself? To make matters worse he was taking her children with him saying that it wasn't right for them to share her unclean state. Her entire world crashed around her leaving her humiliated and in such despair, she didn't know how she could live through it all. Her parents had both passed over and there were no relations that would accept her. She learned days later that Simon had provided for her even buying her a little house on the outskirts of town so she would have a decent place to live out her life. Sadly, he had moved to another town leaving Anna behind. Losing contact with her children was the last straw that held her life together. Nevertheless, she determined to continue to search for a cure willing to do whatever it took to be reconnected to her beloved children.

Anna lived alone on the back of this quiet street for nine long years. It was close to the market and the well. The house was sturdy and well made, over the years, she kept in loose contact with Simon, and he still aided her when needed. The window was a bit unusual in that it sat lower down on the wall than was customary but had good shutters to shut out the weather and the night. To Anna's delight, it allowed her to sit at the table and watch the world go by.

She had little adult company, except for a few kindly souls who if they had the time would sit outside the door or window and visit with her. The other women would come to tell her the news of the area and of any healer they thought might be of help to Anna. The neighboring children on the other hand, would poke their heads in the door and visited with her often. Some children even were coming to tell their woes to a sympathetic ear, which warmed Anna's sad heart.

As the sun sank lower into the horizon, she found herself thinking about her finances. She knew she was getting down to the last of her money both her inherited and that which Simon had provided. She was finding it difficult asking him for more money as he knew she was spending it on cures that never materialized. He had warned her often that the so-called healers where nothing but charlatans and thieves often dressed in respectable clothing. However, she needed to try one last time. She was feeling desperate and fearful for her life, her situation becoming worse as time passed. She couldn't go on without trying her best to keep on living; she was willing to try anything or anyone at this point. Even though there'd been no new healers around in months there were rumors about a man from Nazareth called Jesus. For years, she had prayed for healing or for the bleeding to just stop but neither happened. She had spent so much of her time and resources trying to find some help but all that happened were more pain and no healing. When someone did appear to have an answer for her the anticipation would be almost unbearable and the letdown was a hundred times worse, leaving her in a despairing depression that would last for months. Next appeared anger with both the healer and herself for even believing she could be healed. For Anna she was always thinking that it would be different this time, this time she would be healed. This time she had assured herself she had done everything right and in proper order, so surely God would have an answer for her. She had spent most of her time lately crying out to God she was only 26 years old surely her life wouldn't be ended this soon it just couldn't be. Struggling with her weakness and fear, she still found herself becoming a little more reduced each passing day.

Yesterday, she had stood up and suddenly found herself on the floor with a big bump on her head from hitting the leg of her chair and a splitting headache. The profound realization of her weakness hit her with a savage blow. The resulting despair flooding her emotions, her hopes and faith sinking to new lows as silent tears weld up in her eyes. She lay there on the floor, with her head on her arm, and just simply cried. For so many years, she had pushed away the tears, refusing let go and cry her heart out in her grief and sorrow. She had determined that if she couldn't be strong physically, then she would be strong emotionally, thinking that tears were a weakness, never considering that God had given us tears for the outlet of pain in all its forms. However, she found she just couldn't do it anymore. With little physical strength and the emotional strength slowly leaking out of her, the dam simply broke. The longer she laid there the more she cried, until she was racked with huge shuddering sobs of grief, loneliness, and despair.

As Anna lay there and the tears finally slowed, she thought back to the early days of her marriage. She wondered at the never-ending energy and strength she remembered having. Anna had always been blessed with good health and a strong constitution. As a child she was never sick, she never had the childhood ills, as did most of her playmates. She was also physically stronger, than most of the girls and many of the boys her age. As she grew older she could work for hours at a time and still have energy to spare. There was little she could not do and was often called upon by the older women of their circle to help with some task.

When she had first been sick, she believed that this infirmity would soon simply go away. She fully expected to return to full health in no time, but that didn't happen. Instead, as the days and months passed, she became weaker and weaker. What used to take her minutes to accomplish now took her hours sometimes turning into days. There were times when she would push herself and then have to deal with the debilitating tiredness than always followed. This led to days when she simply couldn't even make her mind work. When she tried to explain how she felt others would look at her with this forbearing pity. Over time that changed to an attitude of get over yourself. They couldn't see her infirmity so many assumed it was her trying to pull them into a pity party. When she was finally forced to lie down during the day and her work wasn't done, the gossip slid from one household to another, branding her as shiftless and lazy. At first, the pain of these not so silent accusations made her push herself even harder. When she finally collapsed, the anger she felt at her body's betrayal had never been so intense. She wailed and ranted at God for doing this to her, until she realized this could not be God's doing but was the enemy of humanity and God's. In those early years, she was often angry, frustrated, and impatient with herself and her inability to do what had always been so easily achieved. She had to fight bouts of depression and was often filled with a resigned self-pity, and despairing fear. As a result, she and Simon had the first arguments of their marriage.

Now, it seemed that her life was ending. There was no more money for healers that didn't heal and her symptoms were getting worse by the day. The fall and the emotional eruption following had drained all of her reserves. However, a few days ago when she had been praying a scripture from Deuteronomy came to mind recalling God's promise of health and wellbeing for His people if they would follow and honor Him as their God. Lying there thinking about it, the more convinced she became that no matter what else happened she had to make a choice. She had to choose whom she was going to believe, either her body or God. She knew God healed for the Torah said He did. Ps. 30:2 It also said that God was her provider, her healer, and her peace. He was everything to her and for her. During these years of sorrow and pain, His joy had been her only strength. Ne. 8:10. She was now more determined than ever to choose to believe that somehow, someway, her God was going to find a way to make her whole and well once again.

Anna determinedly pulled her mind away from the past. This morning she'd heard about this new healer, the one they called Jesus of Nazareth. The neighbor women had been at the well getting their daily water. It was late in the morning and Anna had been surprised to see them still there, talking about this Jesus. Some were whispering that He was the Messiah Himself who would soon free Israel. However, most of the talk most of the talk was about His astonishing ability and willingness to heal any and all who came to Him. The women related story after story of what they'd heard said about Jesus and His ministry. Imagine a man, a carpenter no less, being able to cure illness, sickness, disease, and infirmities! Many couldn't decide if it was the most wonderful thing they'd ever heard or the most ludicrous. At one, point a young girl related how Jesus had healed her cousin of the dreaded leprosy. Sarah her neighbor said, "Anna you should go and ask Him for healing." Anna quietly replied, "I would if I had the money to pay Him. Besides, I'm here in Capernaum and who knows where He is now. I'd never be able to catch up with Him if He weren't nearby. "Then old Mariam reminded them in her rough way that, "He don't call for money He does it for free." Then Elizabeth said, "But I heard that He was here last night. We could ask around and try to find where He stays, if you want."

Anna's heart jumped in her chest as hope once more flared into life once again even stronger this time. Perhaps Jesus could or would heal her! She was at once terrified of believing and at the same time terrified for not believing. Inside she found herself jumping with excitement, wanting with everything in her to believe God had answered her prayers. Could this Man be the answer; could He really be the one? Her fear now was

The Rest of the Story

in not being able to find Him. He could leave town at any point in the day. She might never be this close to Him ever again. But, as her hopes rose, so did the past. Rising up to taunt her were all the old memories of past assurances of being healed, none of which were ever fulfilled. But pushing them aside, she left the women's voices behind her, buzzing with the hope of their friends healing. Emotions of awe, wonder and fear, were all woven through their words and Anna's thoughts. Yet as the day passed, she heard no word that Jesus was still in the city. She had passed the day praying for help to believe in God's word. Hoping with everything in her to hear that He was nearby and would consent to seeing her and heal her.

It was getting dark but no one had come with news she so desperately needed to hear. Struggling not to give into despair, she gave up and simply went to bed. She lay down, truing her best to keep from crying in despair. The high hopes of the day slowly draining out of her heart. Trying to believe, trying to keep from self-pity, while guarding against the thoughts that somehow, she must be at fault and this illness was her punishment was exhausting to her entire being. She struggled to hold on to some shred of hope some remnant belief that somehow someway god would provide a way for her to be healed. Finally, she slept, with one, more tear slowly drying on her cheek.

She woke earlier than usual; sure, she'd heard her name being called. She rolled over believing she must have just been dreaming. Just as she was drifting off to sleep, she heard it again. Her name was spoken by a sweet, gentle voice almost musical in its quality. It was unlike anything she had ever experienced. She struggled to sit up, looking all around, but could see no one that would account for the voice she was hearing. As she moved to lie back down, she heard the words, 'MY CHILD, KEEP FAITH." Stunned, she realized she must have been hearing Jehovah Himself. Awed, she laid back, eyes wide open, trying to comprehend what had just happened. At first, she had a hard time believing God Almighty had spoken to her, her Anna! The words kept repeating in the mind, finally settling deep down in her spirit, bringing her much needed peace. Soon she rose, washed her face, and put on clean garments. Anna slowly got the little bit of housework done for the day and had a bite to eat. At the last minute, she decided to get more water and take a nice leisurely bath in the evening after the sun had warmed the water so she gathered up two jars and headed slowly to the well. Before she arrived, she could hear the excited chatter of the women. Anna wondered at what had them so excited. Sarah saw her first an as Anna neared, she burst out, "He's still here Anna! And I just know He will heal you!" With a sense of wonder in her voice she said," Did you know they are saying the He really is the Messiah?" when Anna was able to ask them where He was staying, their faces fell, as they suddenly realized they didn't know. Turning to each other, questioning, their disappointment turned to frustration and then to anger. Their despair at the disappointment was sharp in the air, as they realized no one had the answers they so desperately wanted for their friend and neighbor. Yet, again in the midst of it all Anna again heard the voice whispering gently, "MY CHILD KEEP FAITH." Shaking her head in quiet wonderment, she turned to the women and softly told them of the morning's events and the words that kept repeating themselves in her mind. In the end, they all left agreeing to keep searching for Jesus. Anna would go home and wait for word while guarding her strength. At that point, several of the women gently relieved her of the water jars, filled them, and carried them back to her home. Each one left her with words of encouragement, some even patting her gently in reassurance. Anna sighed as she went inside, setting her heart to wait for the Lord's provision. For a time of quiet stillness, she looked out the window and prayed for strength, as she looked down the way past the little foot bridge that covered the drainage ditch in the middle of the street. Which often flooded with the spring and fall rains and on down the dusty streets. She decided to cut herself a thick slice of bread and a piece of soft cheese. Sitting down, she slowly ate her meal. Anna sat there again thinking about the past years, the pain, the loss of her children, the social stigma of being unclean, and the ever-present loneliness. She hoped and prayed it would soon be over. She had changed so much, enduring these years of infirmity and being an outcast. She was not the same person. Now when she encountered others with sickness her sympathy and most importantly her compassion rose up inside her, wishing earnestly that she could somehow help. Where she had been impatient, she was now much more patient. The pain and shared feelings of anger, resentment, and helplessness gave her the ability to share the good times and grieve the bad times in a honesty unknown in the past. Even with having to keep her unclean distance. This illness had changed her responses to many of life's realities and she hoped she had become a better person for it.

She must have dozed off because she was suddenly awakened by the sound of a distant crowd. When she had awakened enough to see what had startled her, she wondered at the fact that an event so far away should have awakened her. They were noisy but not much more than the children playing in the street in front of her door or window. Seeing and hearing how the men were loudly trying to talk to each other as well as shouting questions at the young man in their midst. As she watched, the crowd seemed to be constantly in motion, moving like the tide around the young man. He was the only person who stayed in position He was in the center of this group. She sat watching Him as He listened with intensity evident even from that distance. When He answered, He often put His arms around their shoulders as He would for His best friend. She saw that when He was interacting with the people around Him it was with a sense of intimacy that pulled them to Him. The crowd behaved as if they knew He cared about each of them, that He truly understood, and was willing to help. He never turned away, and never left a person wondering where He had gone. She wondered who this could be. She'd never seen a crowd so enamored with a solitary man as they were with this one. Suddenly she knew, and He was coming right to her!

She sat there in wonderment, momentarily frozen, as the reality of the hand of God moving on her behalf sank into her mind and her spirit. Anna was surprised to find herself moving as fast as her body would allow towards Jesus. She was down the steps and half way down the street before the awareness of her situation flooded her mind, stopping her headlong rush towards Jesus. For how was she going to get His attention? How could she even get close? She couldn't just push her way through she was too weak, and she was unclean. No one would allow the unclean to touch them even by accident. Everywhere she went she had to loudly declare herself unclean. She couldn't shout loud enough to be heard over all those men. When she had left her house, she hadn't stopped to think this through. She should have asked one of the other women to come with her but it was too late now. Walking a little further, she crossed the bridge and sank down into the shadow of the little bridge and closed her eyes in prayer. Her mind was hammered with thoughts of discouragement and fear but this time she hammered back. Actively choosing to believe her God would not bring her this far and then fail her. She had already decided that if she couldn't ask Him for healing then she would just need to touch Him even if it was just the hem of His garment.

Even as she crouched, there in the shadow of the little bridge Anna absolutely believed that this time she would be healed. All she had to do was reach out and simply touch some part of Jesus and God would heal her. As she waited for what she felt to be an eternity, while the stones bit into her knees, she prayed she would have the opportunity to reach out and touch Jesus, even if it were for only an instant in time. For she was sure He'd never even notice.

Then unexpectedly, He was there and just as rapidly He was gone, Anna was stunned. This just couldn't be happening, not today, not now! God wouldn't, couldn't let her get so close to her miracle and then snatch it away. Her mind hammered her with thoughts of discouragement and fear but she hammered back. In that moment she actively chose to believe that God would not bring her this far and then fail her. She had already decided she just needed to touch Him even if it was just the bottom edge of His cloak. As her mind screamed at her, 'YOU FOOL! YOU FOOL!" the words she'd heard this morning came back to her, "MY CHILD, KEEP FAITH." The quiet repetition to the words gently drowned out the panicked fear and the savage disappointment. Looking up Anna saw that another group of people was coming to meet Him. They were pushing Him back towards her once more. Abruptly Anna saw her chance. Shaking with fear and fatigue, she pushed herself forward with her last remaining strength. Her slender hand reached out through the legs of the men towering above her and touch the hem of Jesus's' garment.

When her hand touched the material, a shock ran up her arm and spread through her body. A look of wondering, baffled shock crossed her face and then changed to a delighted awe, which held her immobile yet trembling from her head to toe. Finally, she sank back against the wall knowing she had been healed.

Neither group had seen her crouched at the foot of the little bridge. As they had started to pass her, the scribes and the Pharisees had been peppering Jesus with questions, demanding to be heard and answered. The disciples were doing their best to shield Jesus from the crowds. To their frustration, He had been stopping in the streets to talk with anyone and everyone. The problem with Jesus was that there wasn't anyone He didn't take time to talk with and listen to. From the children and babies playing in the streets to the old folks sitting near their doorways, Jesus had a kind word for everyone. No one was ever too old, or too dirty, too rich, or too poor. Even the feeble minded enjoyed His attention. Their infirmities didn't hinder Jesus. He would speak with them all and also healed them all.

Consequently, when Anna touched Him, and He stopped and asked who had touched Him, the disciples were incredulous! How could He ask such a thing? Everyone had been touching Him! Anna tried to discreetly move away from the crowd. She thought she could quietly, disappear and no one would be the wiser. She was astonished that Jesus had asked His disciples who had touched Him! She had barely touched the fringe on His garment. How could He have possibly known? There were people all around Him. Even now, the crowed was jostling Him and He wanted to know who had touched Him? It was madness to even ask such a thing. However, it was apparent that He was indeed very serious so they did try to discern who had indeed touched Him. Nevertheless, Anna too, saw that He was very serious and shaking both from fear and delight at what had happened, she gathered her courage. Turning around, she looked into the gentle eyes of her Savior. She took two small steps and fell at His feet, and suddenly her entire story came pouring out of her. When she was done, He knelt down before her and taking her hands in His, gathered her into His arms. Lifting her face. He said to her, "Daughter, your faith has made

The Rest of the Story

you well: go in peace, and be healed of your affliction." Luke 8:47-48 Helping her up off the ground; He gently guided her through the crowd. When she turned to thank Him, He gently laid His fingers on her lips and addressing her with greatest of respect said, "Woman your faith has made you whole." Again, the tears of relief and thankfulness welled up in her eyes. He gently held her close, letting her cry while confirming to her that her Father had indeed healed her and loved her.

When He left, she hurried home and oh the rejoicing when her neighbors found she had been healed and by that Nazarene Carpenter Jesus. The entire community rejoiced with Anna as the wonder of it all kept returning over and over again washing her with waves of joy and gratitude. She delighted in her growing ability to move and not be exhausted by anything. There had been so many simple things that she had had to leave behind as the long years of sickness and infirmity went by. However, what relived her most was the knowledge that God her Father didn't use sickness and disease to teach or chastise His loved ones. She was indeed free of sin; this past sickness was not her punishment for some error long forgotten. It never did exist. It did however, come from humanities gravest enemy Satan himself. No caring, loving Father, no parent would ever countenance that kind of abuse to his or her child. How could anyone think that the Father of all creation would commit that kind of atrocity on any child belonging to Him? How it must hurt the Father to know that many of His people believed this wretched lie from the pit of Hell.

Jesus was sent to teach and to die so that each of us could know the exquisite love that only He, His Father, and the Holy Spirit could impart to us. Your creator knows and cherishes everything about you. He knows how you think how you feel and how you will act and react. He has known you since the beginning of time and before. Read Psalms 139 for it says *"Your eyes saw my substance, my being yet unformed, when as yet there were none of them."* He continued to love you when He sent His only child His beloved Son to live and die for you. Yes, Jesus died for you, for every single person ever born and was yet to come He died a tortured, agonizing death at the eager hands of Jews and Gentiles not yet His.

Jesus died to not only wipe out our sin but He also died to exterminate sickness and infirmity from all of His Father's beloved children. Your Creator knows, and cherishes everything about you. He has loved you before you even yet existed. He continued to love you when He sent His only begotten Son, Jesus to be beaten and crucified for YOU. Yes, He died just so you could be free of your sin, sin that blocked you from the Father's love and His healing touch. Yes, Jesus died for you, but in the process, He was beaten until He was unrecognizable as a human being. All so, you could be healthy and without sin in His Father's eyes. He loved you so much

The Rest of the Story

that He was willing to go through it all for you. "He was pierced through our transgressions, He was crushed for our iniquities; The chastening for our wellbeing fell upon Him. And by His stripes we are healed." Isaiah 53: 5

STOP right now, right where you are and walk into His arms, and tell Him you believe He is the SON of the MOST HIGH GOD and that you will walk in His footsteps for the rest of your life. Put your head on His chest; let your arms hold Him close. Feel the scars in His hands and in His side where they stabbed Him to assured His death. Let yourself be loved by your MAKER, your CREATOR, and THE LOVER OF YOUR SOUL. He has loved since before time and His love never stops.

AMEN!

MATTHEW 9:9

As He passed from there, <u>He saw a man</u> named Matthew sitting at the tax office. And He said to him, "Follow me," so he arose and followed Him."

Luke 5:27-29

After these things, he went out and saw a tax collector named Levi, sitting at the tax office. And he said to him, "Follow Me." So he left all, rose up, and followed Him. Then Levi gave Him a great feast in his own house. And there were a number of tax collectors and others who sat down with them.

Matthew

When Matthew was a young boy, his father sat at the gates of Jerusalem and was considered a man of great learning and wisdom. Not a day went by that the men of the city did not stop to hear what he was teaching or just listened to his conversations with others. Often he told stories taken from the multitude of scrolls in his private library. He taught his son at an early age to read and understand many histories of Israel as well as other countries of the lands surrounding them. He also taught Matthew his numbers and how to make and hold on to his money. Often he sat at his father's side, as he grew older, listening, and learning from the scholars that surrounded him. As the years passed, Matthew became known for his fine mind and gentle loving spirit. His peers sought him out as a fun loving companion whose contagious smile would win over anyone the boys met.

Matthew's father had many good qualities but even he could make mistakes in business and one failure seemed to just roll out into all areas of his business life. Moreover, as time passed, so did the family's fortune all unbeknownst to them. In the midst of this, His father could have recovered most of the family's wealth and prestige if he had simply sold the treasures of his library. He had often been offered a small fortune for just one of his scrolls. Then came the final disaster, their home caught fire. That day Matthew lost his home, his parents, one sister, and their inheritance, all in a single day.

For Matthew, that day and the weeks following were filled with pain and mind numbing grief. He and his remaining two sisters were now orphans, homeless, and had inherited a massive debt they were incapable of repaying. At nineteen years of age, Matthew found himself unprepared for the responsibility of caring for both himself and his two sisters in spite of all his father had taught him. He had just enough money to feed them and they could stay with neighbors for a short time. At one point in his struggles, he even considered selling himself into bondage in the hopes of earning enough to get them a small amount of financial space to provide at least a roof over their heads. To his chagrin, he found that he would not bring a high enough price to keep his sisters safe let alone repay the debts. Consequently, he took his sisters, and ran from Jerusalem hoping to find some answer to their troubles in Capernaum, away from the constant humiliation and threats of attack coming with the of demands for money he didn't have. They had been there for weeks now and were in desperate trouble, for in two days' time he would be out of money.

There were no jobs to be had that would come close to supporting all three of them let alone pay off the debts.

Yes, he had an education but it depended on money to earn more money and he didn't have any. There was nothing that had prepared him to earn a living from nothing. He and his father had simply believed that he would take over the business after a few years of training with his father by his side. That should have been his next step but it wasn't to be.

He was out walking that last evening deep in thought and worry, when he looked up and discovered where he was. He found himself a little frightened but also curious. This was where the sinners lived their lives. These were people thought to be unacceptable to both the religious leaders and general society. This is where the Gentiles, the moneylenders, the innkeepers who sold strong drink and disreputable wine merchants all lived and worked their trades. Here also lived the ones so steeped in evil they were no longer even judged to be human They were in fact considered to be void of any particle of humanity, they weren't even given the dubious respect of identifying them with animals. They were the tax collectors. Ones who worked for the hated Romans for what they could threaten or steal from the Hebrew people. Just as long as Caesar got what he demanded he didn't care what method the tax gathers used or how much they robbed from the people. As a result, many collectors' became wealthy and fat off the lives of others.

In fact, it appeared from the laughter and music drifting out into the streets that they lived very well indeed. He shook his head, catching himself thinking that at least being a tax collector would be better than begging in the streets. At those thoughts he mentally kicked himself, he couldn't even begin to see how he'd even start such a life. As he turned to go back to his lodgings, he caught movement out of the corner of his eye. Turning he saw a man's lying partially in an alley and on the street. As he approached, he heard him moan in pain, he had bled all over rich robes and a ring was lying in the street near his outstretched hand. It was obvious robbers looking for anything of worth had beaten him. The stone in the ring shot tiny sparks of red light, reflecting the light from the house close by. As he reached down to help the injured man, he pulled away in fear, begging not to be hurt. So as gently as Matthew could, he reassured the elderly man easing him into a sitting position and then easily lifting him to his feet. The old man haltingly gave him directions to his home and suddenly it occurred to him just whom he was helping. Stopping just for an instant, he thought, "If anyone saw me helping this man, no one in town would ever hire me for anything!" Just touching him would make him unclean until he could reach the temple and be cleansed. At that moment, the old man passed out. Since Matthew couldn't bring himself to leave him there, he picked him up and carried him to his home. Matthew rattled the door and stood back waiting for someone to open the door. Abruptly it swung open and he stood there frozen seeing the loveliest girl he had ever imagined. Her cry of pain and sorrow at the sight of the battered and bleeding old man shattered his paralysis. Following her directions, he walked into the house and laid the man on his bed. Soon there were servants milling around, coming, and going as they cared for the elderly man.

Matthew moved away, thinking to quietly slip out the door but the young girl cried out bringing Matthew to a halt. She hurried over and asked his name and where he was living. She thanked him for his kindness to her grandfather, and politely let him out the barred door. Matthew hurried out of the area and back to his sisters, but not having found any solutions to his own troubles. He was satisfied at being able to help someone else in need, and decided to depend on God to answer his needs. He just didn't know yet what it could be.

The next morning walking out the door of the inn, again in search of work, he was stopped by a funny little man with no hair or teeth. When he talked, he spoke so fast it was dreadfully garbled. After asking him to slow down, he was told that the old man he had helped was called Samuel and he wished to speak with him. With some hesitancy, Matthew followed the servant back to Samuels home. The house still bustled with activity, but his now quiet companion brought him back into a room surrounded by shelf after shelf of scrolls. For

Matthew it was like stepping back in time, but instead of his father behind the writing table there now sat the man he now knew as Samuel. When Matthew was seated, he was surprised to see that, although bruised and battered, Samuel eyes sparkled with humor, life, and intelligence. He was regarding Matthew with a steadfast and wondering look of his own. As the years passed, Matthew often returned in his mind to that first meeting, for it seemed to be the beginning of the rest of his life.

As Matthew sat listening to Samuel's quiet voice, he was astonished to hear him offer to pay his family's debts in return for Matthew's kindness of the night before. Matthew had no idea what to say. He wanted on one hand to shout for joy at his family's deliverance and yet at the same time worried what taking the money would do to his life. That and that amount was surely a great deal more than his small kindness was worth. Samuel brushed aside Matthew's objections and again stunned Matthew into confused silence by also offering him his granddaughter's hand in marriage. Then he compounded Matthew's stunned thought by offering him training in Samuel's business and eventually sole ownership of all that Samuel had. Matthew could not take it all in. All of this? All of his problems gone and marriage to a girl he had fallen in love with at first sight? Matthew knew he could be and was sometimes naïve. In fact, he had been teased unmercifully about it growing up, but this was more than even He could believe. As carefully as he could, he simply asked Samuel, "WHY?" Smiling Samuel began his explanation, he told of the deaths of Debra's parents, how he had later lost not only his only son but also his business heir. He told Matthew of lying there in the street believing he was about to die unprepared, leaving everything in upheaval and distress. He realized that his premature death would cause extensive problems for a multitude of people. These realizations had jolted him into an awareness he had found to be very uncomfortable. Samuel had always prided himself on being known a shrewd businessman leaving no stone unturned and always prepared for every eventuality. Samuel was very much aware that if Matthew had passed him by, he would very well be dead and Debra would have been at the mercy of a very unforgiving world. To Samuel this alliance would solve not only a multitude of his problems but also Matthew's, for Samuel was very aware of Matthew's difficulties. Having had one of his men investigate Matthew's situation and his background.

Matthew went back to the inn with enough to pay for another few days and meals, after agreeing to let Samuel know his answer the next day. Walking down the road, he staggered as the full force of the offer hit his mind. He stopped and leaned against the nearest building to hold himself upright. Samuels offer was incredible. A beautiful wife, a job, and the horrid family debt paid off. That mind numbing and hope consuming debt would be paid off, gone forever, all in one moment of time. However, was it all worth becoming one of the most despised men in the country a man considered to be lower than a snake, a hated tax collector, He just didn't know. However, when he returned to the inn he found his sisters crying in the alleyway their belongings stacked around them. The innkeeper had thrown them out and because they had, no more money to stay there, so Matthew gathered his sisters and he returned to the house of Samuel to tell him he would accept his proposition. Samuel and Debra welcomed them with open arms and hearts into their home. For the first time in months, they felt they were safe.

The next day's brought many new changes to their lives. The betrothal was being arranged, the list of Debtors handed over to Samuel, and Matthew's training began. The following year was hard on both his sisters and on Matthew. Knowing in his mind how tax collectors were viewed was a world of difference in actual reality. Soon after the wedding, Matthew was able to locate an uncle in Alexandria who agreed to take his nieces into his home and arrange good marriages for them when the time came. Both girls were delighted to leave Israel for the stigma of Matthew's new profession was a hard burden for them to carry. Yes, they would miss their brother but not the cruel behavior of the rest of their world. Yes, Matthew had endured much of the same reviling taunts, as had his sisters but he was still training and the full wrath of the people was not yet a constant annoyance in his life. What he didn't see, what he didn't yet choose to understand, was how the rest of his world would view his newly found profession. For there would be a steep price to be paid that would haunt the rest of his life, however, that soon changed.

Several weeks later, Matthew insisted on being the one to go back to Jerusalem to pay off the family's debts. He wanted the satisfaction of personally clearing these debts. He had endured the men's taunts, their reviling words, and their utter disrespect for his father and the abhorrent situation. He wanted to face these men hand them the money and tell them what he thought of them and their attitudes. Many of these men had supposedly been friends of the family, and some were not, but it would give him tremendous satisfaction to see the debts erased from the wall. Old Samuel had earnestly tried to dissuade him from doing this. Telling him that the world he knew would no longer accept him as an honorable man. However, Matthew in his sincere stubbornness insisted that he alone must do this and not some servant of Samuels.

Sadly, Matthew was to find that Samuel had been right. Those supposed longtime friends of his family, refused to even take it from his hands. Even some of the servants refused and he had to put the money on the ground for them to touch as if it were grossly tainted. The enemies of his father blatantly delighted in humiliating him. Matthew fought with the realization that men he had known all his life were turning their backs on him, many spitting on him to show their contempt. In his shocked confusion, he finally began to understand the reason for their behavior. However, to him it still didn't make rational sense. Wasn't he still Matthew? Hadn't he sat in their laps as a child? He had played with their sons for all those years. They were his friends; he was paying the cursed debt wasn't he? As the anger and hurt rose up inside him, he thought, they were the ones who had hounded him day and night, never giving him a moment's peace, threatening him and his little sisters until they had to run to a strange city to escape them. He had found the money to repay them, why would they refuse to take from his hand, why the humiliation and ungodly words?

Wisely, Simon had sent his bondservant Phillip, with Matthew to help along the way, which to Matthew had been foolishness, but had agreed to keep the peace. Samuel knew what Matthew would be facing; word had spread everywhere that Matthew had been corrupted by the wicked, godless, tax collectors. Philip was an educated man with a compassionate heart, so Philip was the one who collected the statements of release as they moved from business to business. The money was left with servants or scribes who gave witness to the debt being paid while Matthew stood silently by, humiliation

The Rest of the Story

coloring his face as Philip collected the receipts. They then went to the wall by the city gates where Philip silently handed over the receipts to those whose job it was to record these things. These same men, in whose laps he had sat as a child, refused now to meet his eyes. Most averted their faces, others stared, contempt visibly written in their manner, sneers covering their faces. This public humiliation was the last straw. His pride had been systematically torn to shreds all day long. Now, he felt as if liquid shame, disgrace, and abhorrence were being poured over his head. Stiffening his spine, he stood stiffly upright, staring straight ahead. The elders appeared to wipe the debts form the wall in slow motion. One by one, they were removed, their arms moving as if regretting the deed. The deadly silence alerted the crowd of some detestable occurrence. Matthew was at first scarlet with rage that he could be treated in this shameful manner. Struck equally by shock, and shame he heard the words hissing along the crowded street, like a venomous snake, threading its way closer and closer. At first whispered, it passed from person, to person, and then became louder and louder until they were screaming at him and Philip. All that hatred, held in check for the abomination that was Rome, was now centered on them. The crowd spit the words at him, Tax collector, Tax collector! Repeating the words until it thundered in his ears, and then came the other vile hurtful words. He was called every contemptable, ugly, foul name known to men. Philip took one long look at the crowd seeing the ugly hatred on their faces and knew their lives were in significant danger. Many in the crowd were already reaching for rocks with which, to stone them. He grabbed Matthew's arm and shoved him out of the crowd and down the alley and into a run for their lives. The crowd pounding behind them, until they spotted the Roman soldiers seen coming down the thoroughfare swords drawn. Everyone then scattered unable to meet such a force and live, since they were not allowed weapons of their own by the Romans.

Matthew, was so beaten down by the hatred of his old neighborhood, he could barely function. Philip, seeing the innkeepers face when they came back to gather their belongings for the walk back home, needed no further convincing that it was prudent to leave the city of Matthew's forefathers. They had turned on him, they would no longer welcome him in their midst. His perceived sin was such a blot on the Hebrew nation, that his name would be wiped from their remembrance. He was now worse than the walking dead. He no longer existed. Not even in memory would he be acknowledged. The pain of that reality, of that banishment, twisted in his gut until the force of it felt like it would rip out his insides. What had ever made him think that it would be different for him? He stumbled, gasping for air as he realized he was now considered one of them; he Matthew was a hated and scorned tax collector an abomination to his people. Philip pulled the shattered young man into the cover of some trees and bushes along the side of the street, sitting him down and comforting him as best he could. Tears welled up in Philip's eyes at the intense pain and suffering and had been inflicted on this stubborn but gentle young man.

As the years passed, people's attitudes never changed, Matthew learned the trade but saw that excessive greed and abuse was not needed although it was an excepted practice. The other Tax collectors had come to regard this practice as just recompense for the intolerance and abuse they suffered in their daily lives. When Samuel died and Matthew was now in charge, he determined to do things differently. It surprised him when word began to spread that he was different even better than the others were. They determined that if you had to pay these hated tax's it was far better to deal with Matthew than any of the other Tax collectors. Yes, he too claimed a bit more than the actual tax but as the Romans payed only a pittance to collect these wretched taxes, so to pay for his time he had to have something to make a living. He admitted he had problems with the way things were, so he tried hard to cope with the pain. In recent years, it seemed the pain and humiliation just got worse. He'd give just about anything for others to look at him and actually see another human being. To acknowledge that he was indeed a man, that he loved and laughed and hurt like anyone else, I am more than a dirty word to the rest of the world, but it never happened. Through it all, he never did become greedy, to him it just wasn't the necessity that others saw. Over time, his business grew and so did his family. It broke his heart to separate himself from his children but for their welfare, he felt it necessary to send his growing children to his sister's in Alexandria to complete their education and live their lives free from the general attitudes of the public. The stain of their father's profession would not make them miserable or outcasts, forcing them to strive far in excess of any others to prove themselves worthy. Unfortunately, the people of Israel had no tolerance for either the hated Tax collectors or their families.

Debra was visiting the children when he first heard about the one they called Jesus of Nazareth. He had been hearing rumors for weeks but had never thought they were real. He had caught sight of a man teaching a crowd near the road he was traveling one day and decided to stop and listen. He happened to be returning from an outlying village. Moreover, where the road passed by a large open meadow filled with people listening, sat a man in their midst teaching the scriptures. This took Matthew by surprise for not even the Pharisees spoke with such utter confidence. He looked to be this Jesus just from the general descriptions he'd heard. He was about Matthew's age, maybe as much as 10 years younger but appeared completely comfortable talking to such a large crowd, even with Scribes and Pharisees present with their snide

The Rest of the Story

and sarcastic comments. Matthew decided to stop and listen so he dismounted and sat on the edge of the grass as far as possible from the crowd and still hear what was being said. As he sat there, he found himself wondering if this Jesus ever suffered from the differing beliefs and attitudes. Matthew had tried to be different. He tried not to hate the ones who were so cruel, who tormented his wife and made it necessary to send his children far from Israel. He had seen the bitterness that struck out at others at every opportunity. He believed that this only fed the outrage, and then that hatred fed itself from the mutual pain and damaged everyone, including himself.

Matthew drew in deep breaths of air as the longing for his rightful recognition as a man, for fellowship, again welled up inside, threatening to overwhelm him. When suddenly, looking straight at him Jesus, said, "You have heard it said, you shall love your neighbor and hate your enemy. But I say to you, love your enemies, bless those that curse you, do good to those that hate you, and pray for those who spitefully use you and persecute you." Matt. 5:13.

Matthew was stunned. Questions ran through his mind like sand through an hourglass. How could He have known? Did Jesus know him somehow? Try as he might, He could think of no time where they would have met. They'd never laid eyes on each other. How could He have known Matthew's thoughts and his pain? Questions continued to ring in his head all the way back to his home. In the following days, he went about his business, but the look in the teacher's eyes when He had gazed at Matthew haunted his dreams and his waking thoughts.

Late one afternoon, very close to evening, Matthew was still working outside where he had set up his office under the eaves of his home, both, for the convenience and because it fronted a busy market street. This made him more accessible to people wanting to pay their taxes. When he heard a commotion down the way, he didn't trouble himself to look up to see what it was all about. As the noisy crowd grew closer, he was able to judge from the tone of their voices that it didn't concern him so he continued to finish his day. As they drew closer, he looked up to see a large group with a lone man in the center, everyone talking with him and with each other. Occasionally, He'd hear the somber tones associated only with the pious Pharisee's and Scribes. Thankfully, this time it wasn't the strident call for repentance with the ringing tones of righteous wrath with which the neighborhood was often afflicted. He had often thought the strident calls for repentance was just a convenient excuse to be in the area where all sorts of temptations lived and were available.

As Matthew continued his work, he was again lost in what he was doing. When a shadow fell across his work, he glanced up, and found himself looking into the eyes of Jesus. In those gentle eyes, Matthew for the first time in years saw a man reflected back. At first, he couldn't believe what he was seeing. He looked away and then back to make sure of what he thought he was seeing Jesus was looking at a MAN at him Matthew. Jesus slowly reached out His hand to Matthew and said, "Follow Me." Stunned Matthew slowly stood up and in that moment, the full implication of what Jesus was saying and doing washed over Matthew's mind and heart. Matthew, stretching out his own hand laid it in the hand of his Savior and Creator, and simply said one word, "YES!" Then he smiled the big boyish grin that had once been his trademark. The answering smile on the Master's face looked as though it might split His face in half. Jesus pulled him from behind the table and wrapped His arms around Matthew. Jesus held him close, as with a long lost brother or dear friend. When He pulled back there were tears running down His face and magnificent joy in His eyes. Matthew was astonished to see the depth of this Man's love for him.

Minutes later, Matthew invited the entire crowd in for dinner and sent Philip to inform the cook and the servants that there would be company for dinner. What surprised Matthew was that Jesus accepted the invitation! This was unheard of doubly so because the rumors said He could be the Christ that everyone had been hoping, praying, and yearning for through the ages. This was a man of growing renown, a Rabbi, a true Healer, a Teacher that taught the scriptures with absolute wisdom, understanding, and confidence. Yet, when Jesus looked into his eyes and held out His hand in friendship, Jesus didn't see anything other than a Man. An actual living breathing Man with hopes dreams and hurts so deep his spirit had been curled in a ball never wanting contact with anyone ever again. Instead of a vile abomination, a stench in the nostrils of God, Jesus saw a Man, but not only did He see a Man but He saw a Man that was a child of His Father's hands and He loved him. Matthew watched his guests, as they crowded around Jesus, talking with Him, touching Him, trying to get close. The street children had somehow followed the crowd into the house, and the servants were busy trying to hustle them out. Yet, Jesus stayed their hands and gathered the children to Himself. Talking, listening, sometimes roaring with laughter at what they said, this further delighted the children. He often fed them from His own plate. One after the other, each was attended to. Each child, each man, and each woman, cherished, nourished, and made to know God's exceeding love for them.

Jesus had also done that with Matthew. Oh, He didn't feed him from His plate, but feed him He did. He fed him self-respect, worth, and honor as a man who is utterly loved and valued by his Creator. He fed him the longed for acknowledgement of his humanity. Finally, He fed him with the love of the Father for a beloved child and as this reality fully penetrated Matthew's heart, he broke down and wept with convulsive sobs. However, he soon found himself back in the comforting arms of Jesus with all the pain and torment washed away. Matthew then followed his Master and Lord for the rest of his years.

Jesus is there for you too. He's standing there with His arms open yearning for a chance to hold and comfort you if you'd just let Him. Look into His eyes, see, and know that you are of infinite value to the one who created you. Stand up, take His hand, and let Him bring you into His arms the safest place in the universe. Learn to listen, learn to talk to Him, learn that He will laugh with you and will always be there for you. Learn that He can and will take away all the fear and all the pain that you keep so carefully guarded deep down inside. However, He knows it's there and He knows why it's there, but you don't have to keep it. Give it all to Jesus and never look back. He has willingly taken the fear, the rejection, the abandonment, the anger, and the bitterness. Finally let Him quiet the screaming child on the inside of you that cry's out, "Why, why, am I so alone? Why does no one love me, why does no one see that I am a man, that I am a woman, and that I have value?" Let Him pour His love into that big empty hole inside of you, the hole that demands to be filled! We yearn for something or someone, to fill that aching empty void in our spirit. At some point, we all seem to think that somewhere there is someone or something that can fill it. However,

God made that hole to be filled with Him not any man, woman, or child or thing. Not people, nor houses, nor cars, not food, not drugs, not alcohol, nor all the money the world can produce. We end up invariably disappointed, hurt, guilty, angry, and bitter, as once again this world didn't produce what we needed. Then the inner rage grows and we blame God for everything that is wrong in our lives. We suck other people dry in our frantic attempts to find the right something to fill the hole. Then we cast them aside like a used, up pop can and go on, endlessly searching for that right person or thing to fill the hole.

The truth is, only God is ever going to fill that hole. If you are honest with yourself and are willing to spend the time and effort into digging down into yourself, you too will realize how wrong you have been. Only by letting God and His love, fill that space inside you will you ever be content and have an abundance to give to someone else.

STOP, please just STOP, and let Jesus fill the hole inside of you. He's the only one who can. Please let Jesus do this for you, let Jesus love you! He's right there, right now, looking at you, searching your heart for even a tiny place within you, uncovered by the thick wall and electric fences. He is looking for a way to reach you, a way to touch you. He's already proven your worth and value to Him, He agreed to die for you. Extend your

The Rest of the Story

hand to JESUS and let Him pull you out of that pit of darkness you are in and into His so safe and loving arms for the rest of eternity.

   Go in god's peace, AMEN

MARK 5: 1-20

Then they came to the other side of the sea, to the country of the Gadarenes. And when He had come out of the boat, immediately their came to meet Him out of the tombs a man with an unclean spirit, who had his dwelling among the tombs: and no one could bind him, not even with chains, because he had often been bound with shackles and chains. And the chains had often been pulled apart by him, and the shackles broken in pieces; neither could anyone tame him. And always night and day, he was in the mountains and in the tombs, crying out and cutting himself with stones. When he saw Jesus from afar, he ran and worshipped Him. And he cried out with a loud voice and said, "What have I to do with you, Jesus of the Most High God? I implore You by God that You do not torment me." For He said to him, "Come out of the man, unclean spirit!" Then He said to him, "What is your name?" And he answered, saying, "My name is legion: for we are many." Also he begged Him earnestly that He would not send them out of the country. Now a large herd of swine was feeding there near the mountains. So all of the demons begged Him saying, "Send us to the swine, that we may enter them." And at once Jesus gave them permission. Then the unclean spirits went out and entered the swine (there were about two thousand); and the heard ran violently down the steep place and into the sea, and drowned in the sea. Those who fed the swine fled, and they told it in the city and in the country. And they went out to see what it was that had happened. Then they came to Jesus, and saw the one who had been demon-possessed and had the legion, sitting and clothed and in his right mind. And they were afraid. And those who saw it told them how it happened to him who had been demon-possessed and about the swine. Then they began to plead with Him to depart from their region. And when He got into the boat, he who had been demon-possessed begged Him he might be with Him. However, Jesus did not permit him, but He said to him, "Go home to your friends and tell them what great things the Lord has done for you, and how He has had compassion on you." And He departed and began to proclaim in Decapolis all that Jesus had done for him and all marveled.

Further information can be found in Matthew 8:28-34, and Luke 8: 26-39.

The Testimony

The interior of the cave was dark and narrow. Roughly, carved stone ledges held wrapped bodies covered in dust. The rocks and pebbles that over the years had fallen from the roof lay scattered on the floor. Far in the back, where the air was damp and heavy, a naked man laid huddled on an empty ledge shivering, his emaciated body covered with sores. His hair was long, matted, and tangled yet appeared to move of its own volition. He lay there trying desperately to hang onto his slowly dissolving sanity. His eyes squeezed tightly shut, his mind darting back and forth, searching through the memories of recent days. Josiah watched, as if outside of his body, as he stood and screamed at the night sky, begging to be released from his nightmare of torment. The next instant he saw himself, standing naked on a hillside, jabbering hysterically at a group of people who had brought him food. He watched as he threw rocks, sticks, and whatever else he could lay hands on at the people below him. Finally, the old woman in the group burst into tears and fled back down the path, the others trailing behind her. Moaning he realized that the woman was his family's old neighbor, the one person in their little community that had tried her best to see that he was taken care of. He could feel the shame running down from his mind into his middle where it twisted and burning into this huge gut-wrenching sob of shame and guilty humiliation. He held his head; his moans punctuated by little cries and distressed sobs. Other scenes and their jarring emotions flowed ceaselessly through his mind. He saw his hands scrambling through the rocks as his emotions screamed for an end to the insanity and then his fingers gleefully closing around a shiny, black, sharp edged, rock. Frantically, he smashed it against the nearest stone and razor-sharp fragments showered the ground, grabbing one he cut and slashed his body. Time seemed to stand still, yet streamed by faster and faster until it collapsed in on itself. He found himself lost in another place and time, a place sometimes free of the horrors of his reality, but more often than not, hellish nightmares from which he wouldn't awaken for days on end. When at last he opened his eyes, he knew from the shadows on the rocks that he'd been there a long time reliving the days past. Somehow, he had managed to sleep for a few minutes only to be jerked awake by the hauntingly, sinister, voices. The voices began again pushing at his mind, chittering at him, taunting, condemning, and reviling. The voices grew steadily in volume as they continued to mock him, some simulating the voice of reason, while the others persisted in reproach and vile accusations. No longer able to lie still, he had to move, hoping that just this once, he could leave the voices behind.

Getting up, he staggered to the opening. Blinking rapidly as he came out into the sunlight, he was shocked to hear, and then see, that strangers were making their way up the steep trail through the cliffs. They laughed and joked as they helped each other navigate the last of the trail. The one they called John, flung himself to the ground clutching his chest as if he weren't able to breathe. They all roared with laughter when he came up sputtering from the water one of his friends poured over his head. Josiah instinctively slipped in behind a man-sized rock and was somewhat disconcerted to realize that someone else was also hidden behind the rocks watching the strangers. Since he wasn't automatically attacked, he stayed where he was, watching the men as they emerged on to the plateau. There appeared to be at least a dozen of them. Thankfully, they didn't appear to be the cruel bandits that occasionally sought sanctuary in the graveside caves, forcing Josiah and the others like him to hide further back up in the rocky hills. This bunch seemed harmless enough for the moment, though it never paid to get too close. Josiah nearly jumped from his skin when suddenly, the one who seemed to be the leader swung around and looked right at him. The man beside him gave a shriek of terror and went bounding away into the higher rocks. How this stranger knew that Josiah was there, he'd never know, but He changed his life forever. For some unknown reason he ran to Him and threw himself at his feet. The one the strangers called Jesus began speaking to him. To Josiah the words were strange and muted as if they had a foreign origin or came from a long distance away. In spite of that, he knew they were words of release, freedom, liberty, and were followed by a peace that gently settled into his bruised and viciously wounded spirit.

Josiah found that the closer to Jesus he came, the closer he wanted to be. Contrary to the need in him to come even closer, he suddenly found himself stopping and was astonished to hear coming out of his own mouth the voices that he had believed to be forever trapped in his head. In wonderment, he realized that Jesus was actually conversing with the demons. It took him a moment to understand that in fact the demons were pleading with Jesus to not torment them. Who was this Jesus? These voices were begging and pleading with Him as one who had all power over them. They even were calling Him, "**The Son of the Most High**," imploring Him to release them into the swine that were grazing on the upper meadows. Josiah's mind reeled with the knowledge that someone else recognized their existence. What was extraordinary was that Jesus had total *power* over the demons that had bedeviled him his entire life. For abruptly the demons were gone, suddenly and immediately gone, and he had his mind back! His mind suddenly refused to cope with anything more, and Josiah crumpled to the ground. Slowly he came back to his senses shocked, and intimidated by the number of concerned and somewhat frightened faces encircling him. Andrew, one of the biggest gave him a drink, and then Jesus helped him to his feet. As he rose from the ground, he doubled over again as the realization of his nakedness stained his face with humiliation. One of the other men quickly covered his body with his own cloak this surprising kindness overwhelmed Josiah. Forcing himself to lift his eyes, he found himself looking into eyes filled with tears and loving understanding. He had come to expect condemnation and rebuke, instead he found a friend. Who was this man who was so accepting of him, just who was Jesus? Why and how had He released him from an existence of torment, agony of the mind, body, and soul that Josiah expected to destroy what was left of his life? He had so many questions he didn't know where to start.

For as long as Josiah could remember, he had dealt with the fact that he was someway different. His presence was rarely tolerated. He was looked at as strange and mysteriously dangerous. He'd tried so hard to be accepted but even the leader of their small synagogue wouldn't accept his presence. Even his family left him to his own devices, while the neighbors all shunned his efforts at friendship. All his life he had been so horribly lonely that at times he had wanted desperately to die. As Josiah grew older, he invariably grew angrier. Not just at his family, and the larger community, but also at God. Why had God who had created him, made him to be so completely unacceptable? As he grew in stature, the voices that hounded him since before memory also grew in number and the delusions multiplied. As a child, the town had tolerated him to a certain degree, but as he grew into manhood, they began demanding that he be kept inside at all times. When this could no longer be enforced, the elders had insisted on chaining him to either a post outside his home or later to the city walls. Those days and weeks of abuse and humiliation fueled his rage at his people, and their God. What had he ever done to deserve this? What was it about him that they saw as so inherently evil? He needed help! He needed someone or something to make the voices in his head go away. But there was never even hope to be found. Finally, the insanity and anger gave him the strength to snap the chains and he ran to the only place he could successfully hide; he ran for what freedom he could find in the hills.

Over the years, he gradually moved further out from the reach of the city. He now lived in caves used by the city to entomb their dead. However, as the violence in him increased, the elders of the area of Gadera would convince each other that something had to be done with him and any others like him that were hiding in the caves. They piously declared that people could no longer bury their dead for fear of the insanity of those living in the hills and tombs So they sent out hunters to track them down to be imprisoned by the city, shackled, and chained in pits dug underneath the city. Fouled with vermin, feces, and coldness, that eventually killed you, if the lack of food and water didn't get you first. Over time, he became so adept at escaping so often, that they had finally given up. Now the city elders wanted nothing more than to forget that he had ever existed. Most of them privately hoped he'd die of exposure or of the wounds, he was constantly inflicting on himself in his desperate attempts to drive out the voices of madness in his head.

Jesus the one the other men called Master, held out his hand helping Josiah to his feet. He moved beside him, His arm encircling Josiah's thin shoulders giving him both strength and support. Josiah gratefully leaned on Jesus as they took the trail leading back down to the shore. The friends surprised him by gathering around, helping him when he stumbled and speaking gently to him. They questioned him in their blunt way but they weren't intrusive or demeaning in their questioning. He wondered at their attitude towards Jesus. That they loved and respected Him was evident, but they all seemed to be eying Him with a newfound respect. He caught a certain knowing look that passed between the friends from time to time as they slowly made their way back down the cliff path.

When they reached the shoreline, Josiah eagerly steeped into the water, scooping up sand by heaping handfuls to scrub his body. He couldn't remember the last time he had bathed and from the looks of his body, it was definitely needed. A few of the men pushed the boat out from shore and did some fishing while the others joined him in the water. The fishermen were soon back with the noon meal and everyone had climbed out of the water and was drying themselves when abruptly the one called Peter motioned him to come closer. As soon as he did, the big fisherman pulled out a knife as long as Josiah's forearm. The look on Josiah's face must have been something to see because Peter went from shocked amazement to roaring with delighted laughter. Laughing so hard he could hardly stand, Peter tried to explain that all he wanted to do was cut the matted tangles from Josiah's hair and beard. Finally, with tears of laughter streaming down his face, Peter got him to sit on a log and after frequent stops to survey his handiwork, Peter declared him acceptable. By this time, the fish were cooked and ready to eat. The sight and smell of fresh hot food rolled over Josiah. He wanted to eat until he was stuffed full but knew that if he did in his state of malnutrition, he would end up losing it all. So, making himself eat slowly and taking small bites, He eased through the meal. He held back tears as he unexpectedly remembered other meals he had eaten. He had been alone for so long and the food what there was of it, was always cold, uncooked, or as often as not, unclean. All he had wanted was something to unknot his stomach, something to fill the aching hole in his belly. Jesus once again silently slid His arm around his shoulders and while Josiah briefly hid his face, Jesus gently held him, demanding nothing, and giving everything. Soon they were all eating and talking, quietly enjoying each other and the wonder of the day.

They had all been quietly talking when, from above came a noise like pounding thunder. Although the sky was clear, the earth began to shake, rattling the rock and causing small slides, as the pounding thunder came rolling ever closer. The only one who was untroubled was Jesus. He continued to watch the cliffs, never even moving from His seat by the fire. The rest of the men jumped to their feet and gasped in shock as shrieks and squeals of terror filled the air. Then came the swine, their bodies twisting grotesquely in space, as they stampeded over the edge of the cliffs. The air was filled with the horrifying sounds of their bodies smashing into the water and onto the rocks. Hurling themselves off the cliffs, two thousand pigs died in their mad rush to the sea. The disciples looked on in shocked wonder first at the swine and then at Jesus as their minds began piecing together the events of the day.

From the tops of the cliffs, the shouts and wailing disbelief of the herdsmen broke out over their heads when they saw the shattered remains of their charges.

How were they ever going to explain this? These pigs were for the upcoming Roman celebrations! They and their employers would be ruined! Where were they find enough swine to replace the dead ones, surrounded as they were by the lands of the Jews? Their laments were interspersed with the dying protests of the swine, adding to a pandemonium of noise that could be heard for miles. The shock of it all was too much for the now gentle Josiah and he shrunk down as if to hide in the sand, and covered his head sure that he would be blamed. Unfortunately, his behavior brought the attention of the herdsmen and they began clamoring down the path, very eager to have someone to blame for the catastrophe. Josiah looked up; ready to run, only to realize that Jesus and His friends had surrounded him with a protective circle baring anyone wishing to harm him. Reaching out to him, Jesus pulled him erect and quietly told the eager herdsmen that the Lord God of Israel had delivered Josiah from the demons that had haunted him all his life. That Josiah was now fully in his right mind, and Josiah was responsible for nothing concerning the swine. Several of herdsmen who in the past had hunted him came forth demanding to speak to him and look into his eyes, fully disbelieving Jesus. Claiming that they knew better than any stranger Josiah's true condition. So, Jesus had the disciples move away from Josiah and the main hunter stepped close sure he would reveal their fraudulent claims. No one had been able to do anything about this

The Rest of the Story

crazy lunatic. But when he looked at Josiah, he found a very thin man who for the first time in memory was clean and the mats in his hair and beard gone. When he looked into his eyes, they were as sane as his own, when questioned, he no longer babbled strange nonsense but gave clear concise answers. And finally, he gave up trying to prove Josiah's insanity and backed away, conceding that they were right, he was indeed sane. By this time, the owners of the swine had arrived and seeing that Josiah was innocent began begging Jesus to take His disciples and leave immediately sure that they must have in some way been responsible for this tragedy. Jesus agreed and they gathered up all stray belongings doused out the fire and headed for their boat. As they moved to do this Josiah begged Jesus to let him accompany them. To everyone's surprise Jesus gently refused Josiah's request then holding him close as his eyes filled with tears. Jesus instead told him he had a purpose here that only he could fulfill. He told him to go to all the countryside and tell of his miraculous delivery and that this would honor God Almighty far more than following Himself. So, Josiah humbly accepted this charge and with still tear-filled eyes, and an aching heart backed away as they all got into the boat and prepared to leave. Josiah turned and started the long trek up the cliffs and on his way to the town where he'd been born. Soon he passed the graves of the dead and the living dead. The wonder of his deliverance, the kindness of the disciples, and the loving understanding of Jesus and the Father God had shown him, were all the things that would take a long time to sink into the core of his being. He felt reborn as if in the instant of laying eyes on Jesus, his world, as he had known it ceased to exist and a new one had formed from its ashes. He didn't quite fully know who he was yet but he would find out. Josiah was for the first time truly alive. The insanity was gone. The delusions were gone, and replaced with a sense of peace and security he had never before experienced. He, Josiah was loved. He grinned as he thought about the impact of his testimony. Jesus had wanted him to go to the others of his city about what God had done for him. Josiah was determined that everyone he encountered, would hear the story of what Jesus had done for him!

Do you have a story? I think you do! Oh, it may not be as dramatic as Josiah's or it could be even more dramatic, but you've got a story, a testimony to share with the world if you have accepted Jesus into your life. Really, stop for a moment and think about what Jesus has done for you or would do if you let Him. What cave did you, or do live in? What dead things from your past were or are still haunting you? What had, or has taken up habitation in your body, or in the back of your mind? Past abuse, abandonment, neglect, molestation, rape, drugs, faults, sins, depressions, oppressions, lies about who and what you are. What had or has taken up residence in you? What has Jesus removed or corrected?

The Rest of the Story

Remember His wants nothing more than for you to join with Him and be free of anything that hurts or holds you back from Him and the Father God.

Remember, you will always be a work in progress You not only work out your salvation daily but every day you will discover just a little bit more about this *You,* the person that Jesus loves so completely. Each new day with Jesus, you experience something different to add to your testimony that somewhere, somehow, will touch someone's heart. People need to know that there is *Someone* that will make a difference in their lives, if they just give Him the chance. In fact, He's the only one who can. Don't disregard or belittle your personal story. Know that for someone it is dramatic and very important. It's what Jesus did for you and you alone. Your testimony can and will make the difference to someone else who desperately needs to know Jesus Christ and what only He can do.

Tell your story please; speak that difference into someone else's life! Tell them the Good News; give them your testimony. Go ahead give them Jesus, and you will give them the one thing that will make a difference. Tell them all about Jesus, and what He's done for you. Now!

And go with God's blessing!

Amen!

MATTHEW 27- 28

This is Love

THIS IS A STORY OF THE LAST DAYS OF JESUS, what He may have felt emotionally during this time, and why He agreed to go thru this atrocious experience. When I think of Jesus and what He was willing to go through for humanity I doubt that I truly understand the scope of what He did. Even now I don't think I nor anyone else truly understands the degree of what so compelled Him to agree to go thru with the whole thing, we might think we do, but reality is we barely have even a clue as to what motivated Him to go through it all. We are told He did this just because He loved, but it was a love so incomprehensibly huge in its purity, depth, power, and, it's completely all-encompassing greatness it simply is incomprehensible to humanity. It feels as if that one word should be written across the sky in huge letters but it's not, it's just like all the other words we use daily. Yes, in the Greek there are three meaning to the word love but Agape love is God's love and it just isn't in us to fully understand what it means. It allowed Him to submit to this, it is said that if I or you were the only human being on the earth, He would still have done this for just one person. Apparently, we really are that valuable to Him. He had to not only submit to God Almighty, but to the Priests, Roman law, and finally to the Roman soldiers. He endured the next 24 hours without once crying out, groaning or screaming in pain. Remember Jesus was a man, but a human being who understood who and what He was. He had all the feelings and sensitivities of every man, woman, and child. Nothing passed over Him, He would feel every betrayal, every punch, every kick, every slap, every humiliation, every shame, every bit of pain just as you or I would. Jesus was a man who could have stopped everything with just one word, "NO." Nevertheless, He didn't.

He was not ordinary, not in any way. Remember, He existed before eternity He was there when eternity was created. He created the universes and the whole earth, which He designed and made for us. He came from heaven leaving it all behind, and while here, He worked and lived in total union with His Father and He was one with the Holy Spirit. He was the King of Kings and the Lord of Lords. He was there at the foundation of this planet we call Earth. He was there when everything was created. Imagine what it must have been like to create the first sunrise and sunset, to paint the skies with colors that are so awe inspiring or to watch the fog roll in to water the earth. What man today never having seen fog would

The Rest of the Story

think to water the earth in such a way? Then later call forth the first raindrops to fall, He created the snow fall to cover the earth like a blanket while the earth sleeps, with each flake being unique or placing the billions of stars and planets in multiple universes. Imagine what it was like to create a Lily each one unique, the colors, the shapes of the petals, the scents, and then to give it life, a season and a way to reproduce, then imagine all the other flowers of the earth that He created and that's just flowers not to mention all of the plants and trees and "everything, that has breath praise the Lord." Ps. (150:6). We can do a minute portion of some of these things but we can't give anything life unless we reproduce and that's only because HE made us capable. He breathes life into us, not one human being or anything else is able to do this, we try but often it just doesn't work. When we consider all the worlds His hands have made, down to each minute cell of our bodies, our very hairs on our heads are numbered by Him not just counted but each is numbered so that when one falls, He knows exactly which one it was. It says in Psalms 139 that He knew us before we were even formed in the wombs of our mothers. To give the credit to all this to an explosion somewhere out in the far beyond galaxy feels to me both the height of arrogance and beyond even the minimum of intelligence not to mention just silly. Why, is it so difficult for mankind to admit that there exists someone greater than themselves? Is our arrogance so beyond limitless that when we look at what surrounds us is it not so hugely apparent and obvious that a higher intelligence surrounds us? All our lives we are surround by God. All you have to do is look, really look at what surrounds you, and in fact, look at yourself, there is no one on the face of the earth that is like you, no one in the past, and no one in the future, what else could or would have created the complexity that is you? Then try to convince me there is no God!

This is what and who Jesus is, and what He did, all before He ever stepped foot on this earth. From the moment He was born to this existence He never sinned, not once in all His growing up years nor as an adult. He was perfect. He shared his toys; He didn't hit or hurt His brothers and sisters. He honored His father and His mother, He obeyed his parents, He didn't cuss or swear, or take the Lords name in vain, and He didn't lie, or steal. He didn't covet, and He loved all His neighbors, and He loved His Father God with all of His heart, mind, and soul. He kept the Sabbath, He never murdered not with His mouth nor even thought to do it, nor did He commit adultery, or have any other god before His God His Father. He loved His neighbor just as He loved Himself. Not one of these commandments did He break. He followed the full extent of His Fathers law not just man's interpretation of that law. Always, He did His Fathers bidding, always talking with His Father before He did anything or went anywhere. He was a perfect human being; He was not a human doing whatever came to mind. There was never a time that His Father did not lead Him; there has never been another person like Him ever in creation. He traveled on foot through every town in Israel as His Father led Him, ministering to everyone along the way, healing the sick, raising the dead, casting out demons, and preaching and teaching the multitudes and His disciples every day of His God and His Love for three years.

He then had to face His own death and every imaginable pain that man could contrive that led up to that death. A week before Passover He rode into Jerusalem on the colt that was where He told the disciples it would be. The entire populations turned out to praise and honor Him. "Crying out, Hosanna to the son of David; Blessed is He who comes in the Name of the Lord; Hosanna in the highest! Matt. (21:5,8,9)." How bitter sweet that must have been, knowing what was coming. To His disciples' He spoke of His coming death and how He would die and telling them it was for their own good that He was leaving them for then the Holy Spirit would be sent to them. All the while the crowds shouted, "Hosanna to the Son of David," many of these same people cursed Him two days later and others lied in witness against Him. Jesus then went to Bethany and stayed the night. The next day He returned to Jerusalem but on the way, He became hungry and stopped at a fig tree but it bore no fruit. Jesus made it wither at once. Then Jesus taught them that if you have faith and do not doubt you shall receive. After this He taught many other parables to His disciples. Moving on through the streets He went up into the Temple to again teach and could not bear to see what they were doing in His Fathers' house before Passover. His righteous anger at men who were buying and selling, money changers who were taking every greedy, thieving advantage they could get. He was so very angry and He said to them with a voice of righteous anger that thundered, "IT IS WRITTEN, 'MY HOUSE SHALL BE CALLED A HOUSE OF PRAYER': "BUT YOU ARE MAKING IT A ROBBERS DEN." Matt 21:(12) Tables, then went tumbling over, money flying everywhere, chaos reigned. Money changers screaming at the crowd's, people scrambling and grabbing for the money, hitting and striking out at anyone with anything that came to hand. However, they were soon driven from the temple each one threatening to call down the wrath of God and the priests on Jesus.

When things finally settled down the blind and the lame then came to Him there in the temple and He healed them but once again, the priests and scribes came to Him saying can't you hear what they are saying? Jesus said to them, "Yes; have you never read, Out of the Mouths of Infants and Nursing Babes Thou hast Prepared Praise for Thyself?" Matt. 21(:16) He must have been shaking His head at the blind ignorance of these leaders who were the supposed teachers of God's Holy Word and what it meant to the people. Each day He came back and taught again in the temple and again the priests and scribes challenged Him, but He continued to teach, explaining to the disciples His ending and His return. He unceasingly continued to teach and to minister to the people. Nevertheless, always the Priests and Pharisees followed Him constantly, trying to trap Him into saying something evil so that they could accuse Him. They were like hornets constantly buzzing around Him seeking some way to demean or dishonor Him. After harassing Him for years, months and then daily, He finally turns to them and directly strips their veils from them exposing them to the throngs of people following Him. Telling them exactly who and what they were and their coming judgement before God Almighty. Infuriated Jesus turns to them and begins reprimanding the chief priests and elders of the people who then left and came to Caiaphas to plot together to kill Jesus. Judas also came before the chief priests at that time and volunteered to betray Jesus for 30 pieces of silver. Matt. (23) Judas was one of the twelve disciples that believed that if the authorities did arrest Jesus that He would then be forced to rise up in all His glory and manifest God's kingdom here on earth, freeing the Hebrew people of the tyranny of Rome or anyone else; believing that the Messiah and the disciples would then rule over Israel and the world. Unfortunately, for Judas this was not the kingdom Jesus was teaching and he continued to look for a good time to betray Him. Matt. 26:14, 2 Imagine yourself, knowing that your friend and the people of power in your government today were plotting your death and you knew it. How would you react? Would you be angry, insulted, terrified, or would you be scrambling to grab everything you owned planning to run as far and as fast as possible? Jesus did not run anywhere; He continued to teach in the temple to all the people who would listen. He gave them the signs of His return, He warned of the perilous times to come and His glorious return, He warned them to be ever ready for no one, not even He knew when that would be. Only the Father God would know the day and time. While His heart was grieving Jesus kept on teaching.

Later that afternoon in a room was set aside for their Passover Supper and remembrance. The disciples worked to arrange for the food and everything else that would be needed to celebrate this Memorial Holiday. A room was set aside for their Passover supper which was to be Jesus' last. That evening when He came into the room instead of sitting down and being served, He served them by washing their feet. John 13:5 This chore was always reserved for the least of the household whether they were child or servant. The disciples were astonished that He would do such a thing, but He insisted and washed the feet of each one, again teaching them the ways of God. During this time of fellowship, He continued to pray for each of them, praising and thanking God for each person given to Him. After supper He took the bread and the wine instructing them and us to remember His death for all time. An agony of decision must have been going thru His mind as He broke the bread and poured out the wine knowing that that same reality was soon coming to His body, to be the sacrifice, broken, torn, and bloody that His life's blood would be poured out onto the rocky soil of Jerusalem. Matt. 26:(26-50.

Rising from the table, He took them to the Mount of Olives and there in the garden of Gethsemane He asked them to pray with Him. They tried but were so tired they couldn't quite do it and they fell asleep three separate times. He was then left all alone, fighting His flesh that was screaming at Him to not allow this reprehensible, ugly, foul thing. He fought so hard with His own flesh that the capillaries under the skin of His face, back and chest burst and the blood mingled with His sweat and tears. His flesh telling Him over and over, He was the King of Kings and screaming the question of how could He allow His Holy body to be beaten and torn until He was unrecognizable as a human being? What He also feared in addition to the physical agony however, was the disease and the sin of the humanity. This was something He had never experienced, not once in His Life. He saw what sin did to other human beings how it had left huge gaping holes in their spirits, their minds, and sometimes their bodies. Leaving infected scars, and gaping wounds so filled with putrefaction, corruption, decay, and rotting odor that they could barely live with themselves let alone other people. Sin that humiliated, shamed, and belittled and then was repeatedly inflicted on others. Innocents, children burned alive by acid, torn from their mother's womb, because their parents were afraid or didn't want them. Children sold into slavery by and for perverted sexual use. Children ripped from their parent arms to be thrown into fires of death, their screams muted by the screaming joy of onlookers savoring, and regaling in their pain, the sin and damage of neglect and abandonment. Girls and boys abused by their fathers, mothers, brothers, husbands and wives, some even by their own sons and daughters. Women and men, boys and girls beaten down by fists and words that beat and killed emotionally, as well as physically until their spirits shrank so far down only the hand of God could restore them. People to whom the word love was some vague emotion held by others, or something so small and delicate it couldn't live in the light of day, always needing to be hidden way down deep inside never to be exposed for fear of damage. People reveling in watching others put in cages or arenas to fight to the death from supposedly safe partitions or behind walls that they believed could keep them safe. But the damage to them was multiple; watching as others are killing and torturing others simply for the perverted joy of it, or because of the color of their skin, where they were born or because they looked different; wars that annihilated whole groups of human beings because they were different. In the past, it was called revenge and now it is often called sport.

This was so incredibly hard for Him to comprehend, hadn't His Father created everything and everyone. So, what if they were different, so what if they were born here or there, a rose is still a rose whatever its color, wherever it came from. Whether it's from the forest or the valley it's still a rose, God's creation. Who was humanity to think it had the right to judge a persons' worth or value, everyone belonged to God just as they did. Humanity started out with greedy, prideful, disobedience, then went to vengeful murder and finally to complete and total self-centered narcissism. Sin and its depravity ruled the world and destroyed man's relationship with God the Father; it had to be stopped. The only way this could be done was for Jesus to take it all, every bit of the hatred, vanity, greed, every ugly sin imaginable, onto and into His Holy innocent body, mind, and spirit all because He loved us. He allowed Himself to be the sacrifice, the ransom for humanity. We have no conception of the sheer amount of Love that Jesus had to call forth from deep inside to be able to be the needed sacrifice that would eliminate forever the chasm between Mankind and God Almighty that sin caused. Just the weight of one person's sins would be staggering but to take on all of humanities sin from the beginning of time until its end, it defies understanding, or even a minute portion of our comprehension. Jesus begged God to take this sacrifice from Him. His anguish and despair were so great that the blood and sweat rolled down His body with His tears. Begging His Father to find another way, but even in His asking and pleading He knew the answer, He knew the answer from before the foundation of the world that there was no other way. He must die in the most shameful, humiliating way, but even more He must take on the hurt, the pain of every human being ever born. He was to feel the shame and anger of being raped, of being ripped apart by acid in their mother's womb, of dying by the hand of a loved one, of being murdered. Greed, buying and the selling of His body, being lied to, to be falsely accused, to be beaten, and in addition to all of that agreeing to take on every disease and aliment of mankind into His perfect body; a body that had never even dealt with the common cold. To have COPD to have Cancer, Leprosy, Polio, Shingles, MS, ALS, and Plague disease, to have His internal organs shut down because of damage, to be blind, to be deaf, to have His limbs so damaged they couldn't do their job, to have His body tearing Him apart with every affliction and disease known to mankind. It took everything in Him and in His Father to not say NO!! I will not, I cannot do this, it is too much. Father God took that moment in time to remind Him of *His love for Him*, for the rewards coming from His sacrifice. Bloody sweat streaming down His face, He compelled His flesh into obedience and said Yes, Father; His love for us being so beyond our complete understanding. For to Him we were somehow, someway worth this magnitude of sacrifice. God wrapped Him in an all-encompassing, never ending Love. He was safe in the love of His Father, He had everything He needed contained in that Love. He was willing to die if it were for just a single one of us, He was willing to go through all of it so we could have fellowship with our Father God and share with Jesus all that was His, rewarded to us forever.

The Roman soldiers then came to the garden looking for Jesus of Nazareth. They confronted Him, their attitudes demeaning and contemptuous. But after the first time of Him telling them "I am He" they all fell down before him. Judas then betrayed Him with a kiss on the cheek. How hurtful that alone would be. Try to imagine how you would have felt if your friend did that to you. Even if you knew beforehand that this might happen there would be in me this little tiny hope that it wouldn't. Peter tried to stop it with just his one sword cutting off the ear of the priests' slave. Jesus stopped it all before anyone else was hurt, healed the servant and gave Himself over to them. Saying to them, "If you seek me let these others go." John (18:8) so the Roman soldiers bound His arms and with the officers of the Jews led Him to Annas first, father-in-law of Caiaphas who then questioned Him about His teaching and the disciples. When Jesus answered a soldier of the priests hit Him asking Him, "Was that the right way to answer the High Priest?" Jesus said, "If I have spoken wrongly, bear witness for the wrong, but if rightly why do you strike me?" John18: (22-23) Annas then sent Him bound to Caiaphas who questioned Him again. Here He was found guilty of Blasphemy, for He truthfully admitted to being the "Christ by saying "Yes, it is as you say." Matt. (26:63) He then was sent to Herod who questioned Him extensively but could find nothing to accuse Him for. So, he was sent to the Praetorian and Pilate came out to them and asked, "What accusation do you bring against this Man?" The priest answered saying He was a criminal and Pilate told them to take care of Him yourselves, but the Priest answered by saying, "we have no right to execute anyone." (John 18:31) Pilate left again and came back telling them that they could choose who they wanted killed and he gave them the choice between a robber Barabbas, who had been terrorizing Israel with murder and inciting the people to rebellion or Jesus. They choose Barabbas, and Jesus was led away to begin his journey of savage pain, despair, agony, and death. John (18:38-40) The Roman soldiers then stripped Him of all coverings leaving Him naked fully intending His humiliation, and shame. They put a red robe on Him, and gave him a staff, and then taking the staff, they began beating Him. Next holding Him upright they began punching Him as hard and as heavily as they could, kicking Him with their iron covered sandals and beating Him with their fists over and over again. Others had grabbed vines of thorns and wove them into a crown which they had slammed onto His head. Thorns two and three inches long slammed into His skull the thorns ripping through flash as they "arranged" the crown. The soldiers were enraged because He wouldn't beg or plead with them to stop, nor did He make any sound so they continued to beat Him determined to make Him cry out. They tried making Him speak by pulling out handfuls of this beard, and pulling out his hair. You men who have beards know what it's like when a baby's fingers tangle in your beard imagine someone ripping it out of your face.

They did this all before the whipping and while they tied Him arms high above His head and pulled until He hung from the bar and was barely able to support Himself on His feet with his legs spread and tied down to anchors embedded in the ground. Then all became quiet except for the sound of iron shod boots walking up to the platform and then came the sound of the soft slither and rattle of the whip as it was set to do its job. Jesus cringed inside trying to prepare for what was coming. Nine pieces of tanned leather hide all of varying lengths but each tipped with pieces of iron, pointed barbs shaped to cut and to slice through the skin, the muscle, to tear and rip tendons and ligaments, to shred skin until it was a mass of raw meat. Another man stood to the side to count each stroke; the worst Roman traditional punishment was 40 strokes but only 39 were ever administered for if there was a miss count the executioner would himself received the full 40. Many men had died after 15 lashes very few ever survived the full thirty-nine.

The whip master began yet never hurrying; slowly but constantly and consistently hitting Jesus not leaving an inch of skin intact, from his neck to the backs of his calves and not just what was visible but the inner thighs and down his ribs and abdomen His entire torso, until the 39th lash of all nine pieces of leather stopped. His blood running down His body and each piece of leather as it dripped onto the platform. Jesus never uttered a sound during the entire time but the pain was beyond human understanding. Many had simply passed out from the pain. For Jesus with every stroke of the beating were nine more diseases that Jesus took into His own body. The whipping beat every category of sickness ever known to mankind from before time until the end, into Jesus. Is. 53(5) When they cut the ropes, they weren't gentle, He came crashing down, as His body was no longer able to support Him every inch of skin ripped and torn yet He never uttered a sound. But slowly, awkwardly He tried to stand, finally He was held up by the hard, unforgiving strength of the Roman soldiers. They first dressed Him in His own clothes then drug Him out into the street still bleeding and shaking demanding He carry the beam for His own crucifixion. Luke 23: (26-30) Yelling and whipping about them as they moved thru the crowds out of the gates of the city to Golgotha the city dump. But Jesus was unable to carry it the entire way; the burden of the cross beam and humanities diseases were too much and another was chosen to carry it for Him. Soon He would know another burden and His mind shuddered away from the vastness of the thought. The cross beam crashed down onto the rocks, nearby were three holes dug into the rocky soil, the tall beams ready to receive their burdens. There they again stripped Him of all covering. The scent of human waste covered the area causing eyes to water and people to cover their noses' and mouths,' against the stench. They pushed Him down hard tying His hands to the cross beam first and then pounding the spikes into His wrists. He gripped His hands so tightly His fingernails left half circles bleeding in His palms as He fought against screaming in pain. They then moved the cross beam across the rocks and dirt to the tall beam set to go into the ground. They then nailed the cross beam to the tall beam that would soon stand in the ground just a few feet away. They then moved His tied feet and cinched them down into place so He couldn't escape the nails. The wood scraped the mutilated flesh on the backs of His arms, His back screamed in agony as they forced Him against the wood, long splinters of wood catching in the fleshly ruins of His back, legs, and buttocks. At that point, they pounded the nails into His feet, forcing His knees up at a 35-degree angle to prolong death and suffering held in place by the ropes. The soldiers then came together and laughing took a piece of wood that had been written on by Pilate who wrote "Jesus the Nazarene, King of the Jews," Matt. (19:19) and nailed it above His head. At that point the tree was jerked up by the soldiers and then allowed to slam down into the hole. The anguish that ran through His body was incomprehensible, for at that same moment He felt and knew the Sin. The huge, monstrous, ugly, SIN of all of Mankind slammed into His body. It was about three pm and the sky darkened and stayed that way until the ninth hour. During those six long hours He gave instruction to John for the care of His mother. He also talked with the man hanging beside Him and promised to see him in Paradise. A little later He lifted His head and cried out in voice so full of despairing anguish, "MY GOD, MY GOD, WHY HAVE YOU FORSAKEN ME?" Matt. 27:(46). Later, Jesus told one of the soldiers He was thirsty and instead of water they gave Him sour wine on a branch of Hyssop, soon afterward Jesus said, "Father unto thy Hands I commit my Spirit." Luke 23:(46) And He breathed His last. To make sure He was truly dead the soldiers shoved an iron spear at an angle into His body ripping through vital organs, and His last blood and water gushed out onto the dirt at the foot of the cross. John 19:(34) At the ninth hour, the veil of the temple was torn in two from top to bottom and the earth shook and rocks were split. Matt. 27: (51-53) NO longer was there any separation between God and man, Jesus now stood in the gap, He was the sacrificial Passover Lamb, Jesus was the Ransom for humanity.

The Story however, doesn't stop here. His body was taken from the cross and was cared for and put into a Tomb. To be sure, no one could steal the body Pilate had a huge stone rolled in front of it and soldiers set to guard the tomb. Jesus with all of the sin and disease riddeling His body descended into Hell, where He came face to face with Satan himself and He took all of the sin and all of the disease and shoved it back in Satan's face. Satan couldn't hold Him down or Keep Him there. In hell there, was much gnashing of teeth and wailing by all the minions of Hell for they had been defeated again.

After the third day Mary Magdalene went to the tomb to discover that the stone had been rolled away and she was grieving anew and ran and told the disciples what had happened and they returned to the tomb and indeed it was empty but Mary reminded there grieving and an Angel told her He had arisen and was alive and to go tell the disciples that He is in Galilee waiting for you. Matt:28(5-7) He then gathered them all together and gave this commandment, "All authority has been given to Me, Go, therefore and make disciples of all the nations, baptizing them in the name of the Father and the Son and the Holy Spirit. Teaching them to observe all that I commanded you; and lo, I am with you always, even to the end of the age." Matt. (28: (18-20) He then ascended into heaven and the disciples returned to the upper room in Jerusalem to await the Holy Spirit of God. He then later declared to John in Rev. 1:(8) "I am the Alpha and the Omega the first and the last, and the living One; and I was dead, and behold I am alive forevermore, and I have the keys of death and of Hades."

While I was writing this story, the verses of this song by the Bee Gees, which came out in 1967 the year I graduated from High School, kept playing over and over in my mind. I'm sure you've probably heard them in the background to TV commercials. "You don't know what it's like… You don't know what it's like… To Love somebody, to love somebody, the way I love you." I think that covers the question of why He would allow Himself to go through the horror of His death. I truly don't believe we will ever really and truly understand His Love for us until we sit at His feet. I'm just so glad He does! AMEN!

I had a very hard time with this story. All my life at every Easter I would hear the story of what was done to My Jesus. I got to the point where I just didn't want to see it or to hear about it, it was too ugly and my very vivid imagination could give me nightmares for weeks as a child. As an adult I just refused to go there, I wasn't going to think about any reality of His death. Until God said to me one night as we were talking, write the story

The Rest of the Story

of what happened to Jesus in the two days before His death. Write about how He felt, tell the facts of what happened, but also tell them what He felt step by step and why He allowed it all to happen. I admit my first reaction was out right NO! I just couldn't do it. For days, I went back and forth but my fear of seeing His reality grew until I was ready to panic at the whole idea. It was hard, because God doesn't just tell me what to write He shows me. It's like watching a movie with my eyes sometimes open and sometimes closed. It's as if God had a camera on the scene every step of the way. It's graphic to say the very least. I not only see the people and what they go through physically, but I can hear their thoughts and read the expressions on their faces. But now it's done and I hope when you read the story you will really think about what He allowed to be done to Himself. What He allowed, all He was willing to suffer, the extreme agony of mind, body, and spirit. All just for you and for me. It's called LOVE but it's a Love that we can just barely begin to understand.

Its' not our simplistic concept of love. Ours is rarely that unselfish, that unmotivated by a world of something elses. God's love for us is so comprehensive, so vast, and impossibly pure we can barely understand let alone mimic what is His alone. Yes, it was LOVE but it is God's LOVE and He loved us enough to send His only Son to live and die for each of us. For He doesn't want anyone to perish, that means He doesn't want you to go to Hell for eternity. You believe there is no heaven or hell well think again, God doesn't do things like this for no reason. Just think for just a moment about the idea that you just might be wrong and God is right. Do you really want an eternal existence without God in it? Come on, think about it, no love, no compassion, no kindness, no peace, no faith, no grace, no mercy, no beauty, and no joy. God has surrounded you your entire life. Oh, I know many say that there is no God but they are wrong, for once in your life put aside your great intellect and your oh, so infallible logic, and just simply look at what's around you. Not what man has made but what God made. He is in the very breath you breathe, He has surrounded you from before you were conceived and has been right there under your nose ever since. So where do you want to spend eternity. With Him, or without Him, it will be your choice to the end.

Please take all this and apply it to yourself and all those you care about. GOD'S BLESSING AND PEACE BE WITH YOU AS YOU TRAVEL THIS ROAD.

Sincerely, NANCY A. PARKS

Made in the USA
Coppell, TX
16 December 2021